Hot Line

ALISON GREY

Ylva

Hot Line
© by Alison Grey

ISBN epub: 978-3-95533-015-6
ISBN mobi: 978-3-95533-016-3
ISBN pdf: 978-3-95533-017-0
ISBN Paperback: 978-3-95533-048-4

Published by Ylva Publishing, legal entity of Ylva Verlag, e.Kfr.

Ylva Verlag, e.Kfr.
Am Kirschgarten 2
65830 Kriftel
Germany

http://www.ylva-publishing.com

First published in Germany under the title *Richtig verbunden* by
Ylva Verlag, e.Kfr.

First English Edition: February 2013

Credits
Translation by Sandra Gerth
Edited by Judy Underwood
Cover Design by Krystel Contreras
Cover Photograph: © Candybox Images | Dreamstime.com
                 © Vkoletic | Dreamstime.com

Acknowledgment

I want to thank the wonderful people who helped getting *Hot Line* published.

Sandra—for translating *Hot Line*. I would have taken much longer and probably driven Jae insane.

Jae—for doing a marvelous job as my editor.

Judy—for your attention to detail as a copy editor.

Susanne and Marion—for being patient test readers.

Erin—for beta reading.

Krystel—for creating yet another brilliant cover.

Astrid—for being a dedicated publisher. I wouldn't want to have your job for all the money in the world.

Girls, you're awesome!

Dedication

For Astrid. The best publisher you could wish for.

Author's note

This novella is set in Germany. To help you understand Christina's situation better, here's a short explanation about the German school system:

A "Hauptschule" is a one of three types of secondary school in Germany. Usually, students who don't have good grades in elementary school will attend Hauptschule. The graduates go on to do an apprenticeship or work minimum-wage jobs. They have the option to later attend an evening school or another type of second-chance education to get their "Abitur," a diploma that qualifies them for better paying jobs or university admission.

Hot Line

"Hi, this is Chantal. Thank you for calling," Christina breathed into the phone.

"Um, hello," a female voice said on the other end of the line.

Christina furrowed her brow. Women rarely called her. Not that she would have minded. She even preferred female callers because women usually didn't become obscene. The calls also lasted longer, so they were more profitable for her. At least that had been the case with the three calls that she'd gotten from women since she'd started working for the sex hotline four months ago.

"You're calling at exactly the right time. I'm just undressing to take a hot bath." Christina made her voice sound as if she were revealing a secret. "Do you want to join me?"

"Would it be all right if we ... if we just talk?"

The woman on the other end of the line didn't seem aroused. Christina got the feeling that this caller wasn't interested at all in her "service." But then why was she calling a sex hotline at two o'clock in the morning? "Baby, you can do to me whatever you want." That sentence, presented in her low voice, always excited her male callers.

"I don't want to do anything to you. But I'd like to tell you about my day."

Christina lifted her brows. That was a game she hadn't encountered before. *Okay, why not?*

"What's your name?" Christina still used her sexiest, most seductive tone.

"Linda." The caller's voice sounded young.

"Okay, Linda, tell me about your day, honey."

A sigh filtered through the line. "It's my birthday today. Well, yesterday, really."

"Oh, so happy birthday." It wasn't the first time callers told her it was their birthday, hoping they wouldn't have to pay. But women were rarely that naïve.

"Thank you. I ... I'm twenty-nine now. "

Christina grinned. So she'd been right. The caller was young. She sounded even younger than twenty-nine. *If she's even telling the truth.* It didn't matter anyway. Twenty or eighty years old, on their birthday or their golden wedding anniversary like one of yesterday's customers, they all brought in money, as long as Christina kept them on the phone long enough. "And? Did you have a nice party?"

It took a long time for Linda to answer. Finally, she said in a low voice, "I spent the whole day at the cemetery. When I got home, I wanted to get drunk, but then I changed my mind and stared at the bedroom wall for the rest of the night instead."

Wow, this woman had some serious problems. But why was she calling a sex hotline instead of going to see a shrink? Christina shook her head. Every minute earned her two euros, so she might as well play phone shrink. "What were you doing at the cemetery?" Christina allowed herself to speak in her normal voice. This caller, Linda, if that was even her real name, definitely wasn't interested in phone sex. Or if she was, it was a really perverted version of it.

"My parents are buried there. They ... they died exactly four years ago. They were on their way to see me for my birthday." Linda sucked in a breath. "A truck driver fell asleep at the wheel and crashed into the tail end of a traffic jam. Exactly where my parents' car was." After pausing for a few seconds, she continued, "They never had a chance."

Christina avoided imagining how the woman at the other end of the line might feel. In her job, she had learned to keep feelings out of it. "I'm very sorry."

There was no answer.

"Do you have any siblings?"

"No." Sobbing quietly, Linda said, "It was just my parents and me."

It was probably a mistake to ask so directly, but Christina was just too curious. "Linda, why are you alone today?"

"Because I don't have anyone." The caller's voice broke.

Shit. Is she crying? Christina pressed her lips together. What was she supposed to do now? She was a phone sex worker, dammit. Not even her sisters talked about their problems with Christina because they thought she was insensitive. "Hey, Linda. Don't cry. Everything will be fine."

Linda blew her nose and then said, "I help people."

Huh? "What do you mean?"

"I'm ... I'm a therapist. A psychologist."

What does that have to do with anything?

"I work with people every day. I have my own practice. I leave for work early in the morning and I've got appointments scheduled until the evening."

A shrink and a workaholic. Was she telling the truth? And why was she telling Christina all of this? Was she trying to show off?

"I have no family and no friends. No one. Not even colleagues."

Slowly, Christina realized what the caller was trying to say. "And why's that?"

For a moment, only Linda's breathing filled the line.

"I don't know."

Come on. Christina shook her head. A therapist who didn't even understand herself? "Really?"

"Since I'm a therapist, I guess the excuse I don't like people doesn't work, huh?"

"No, it doesn't." Christina laughed.

Linda exhaled. "People just scare me. It's so easy when I interact with them on a professional basis. I like helping them, giving advice, guiding them to find the right way. But work is one thing. Meeting them in my private life is another."

All right, then, but none of that had anything to do with phone sex. "Why did you call me?" Christina asked.

Linda laughed humorlessly. "It's like you said earlier: I can do with you whatever I want."

Christina moved the phone away from her ear and stared at it. The answer had caught her by surprise. After a moment of silence, she cleared her throat. "What do you want to do now, Linda?" She deepened her voice. The role of Chantal was her safety line.

"I want to imagine you holding me."

"Okay," Christina said. "That's exactly what I'm doing right now."

"Except for handshakes, I haven't been touched by anyone in over a year."

Christina furrowed her brow. This woman had to be incredibly lonely. "I'm holding you tightly." She tried to sound as compassionate as possible. *Poor woman. She's telling the truth. No one could make up something like that.* Why hadn't she hired a prostitute? She could at least let herself be held if she didn't want sex. If Linda was even into women. So far, nothing had indicated that she was. Or that she wasn't. *Doesn't matter one way or the other.*

"Thank you. Whatever your name might be."

"My name is Chantal."

"My name is Linda, but I'm fairly sure yours is not Chantal. I understand that you don't want to tell me your real name, but please don't lie to me."

Christina was silent. Then she heard herself say, "Christina." *What are you doing? She's a customer.* She jumped off the bed, plodded over to her desk, and dropped onto the chair. It creaked even more loudly than usual. This was the first and definitely last time she ever revealed her real name to a customer. It was too personal. Now Linda was talking to her, to Christina, instead of a cybersex slave.

"Nice to meet you, Christina."

Silence. Christina had already said too much.

"I hope I'm not boring you to death because I'm planning to talk to you for a while longer."

Christina grinned. Who cared what they talked about as long as it was lucrative. "Okay."

"I don't have anyone. I just have one thing: money.

I don't care if it costs me three cents or three euros a minute. I like your voice. Your normal voice. And I like talking to you. So if I don't bore you to sleep, I can do that as long as I pay you. Well ... until you finish work for the day." After a moment of silence, Linda asked in an almost shy voice, "How long are you working tonight?"

Christina leaned back in her chair. "Normally until four or five. Depends on how busy it is. But there are no set working hours. We can talk for as long as you want." It would be a very lucrative night. Christina slipped out of her house shoes and put her feet up on the bed.

"Just tell me if you get tired."

"I doubt it."

"Why?"

Damn! First, she revealed her real name, and now she had slipped again. "Just a feeling."

"I asked you not to lie to me." Linda sounded annoyed and disappointed at the same time.

How did she do that? Linda was definitely a therapist. She was coaxing more information out of Christina than she had wanted to reveal. But her insomnia was not a good topic of conversation for a customer. This call was already getting out of hand. "I don't want to talk about it."

"Okay, as you wish." Linda sighed. "Then tell me what you look like. I mean ... what you really look like."

Enough. Linda was violating all of her rules. Christina tried to sound friendly, but determined as she said, "If you want to have phone sex, we can do that. If you want to talk about yourself, we can do that. You called Chantal. And now you want to talk to Christina. But that's not how this works."

Linda kept silent, and Christina was almost sure she would hang up. But then Linda inhaled and said, "Okay, then I'll talk to Chantal."

Now what? What the hell does she want from me?

"Chantal, tell me what you look like." Linda's voice had changed. Now she sounded more distant.

Christina clutched the coffee cup on her desk with her left hand. Her index finger drummed a staccato against the porcelain. Should she pull off her usual act? Even though she had talked normally to Linda the whole time? *I just wanted her to stop asking questions.* On the other hand, she was in her element in her role as Chantal. In a low, sexy voice she said, "I'm five feet eight and very slender. I've got long, blond hair and unbelievably big tits." At least the hair color was not a lie. Her customers didn't want to know that she was only five foot six, weighed one hundred and sixteen pounds, and had shoulder-length hair.

"What color are your eyes?" Linda asked softly.

"Blue." Her green eyes weren't interesting, so that was her standard reply.

No reaction from Linda.

"Do you want to know what I'm wearing?"

"Nothing, I'd guess," Linda said.

Something rustled on the other end of the line. Was Linda eating chips?

"Do you like what you see?" Christina asked, her voice husky.

"For an illusion, I'd say you look pretty good."

Is that supposed to be funny? Ah, to hell with that. Get on with it. "One thing is not an illusion, and that's my voice. I can use it for a lot of things if you let me."

Silence.

"Honey, tell me what you're wearing."

"Since facts don't seem to matter, let's say ... nothing."

Christina tightened her grip on the phone. She wanted to tell Linda to go to hell, but she was a paying customer. *Go on. Ignore her. Just think about the money.* "Okay, now that we're naked, maybe you want to get comfortable in your bed?"

"We can do that, but I have to warn you. I put on my Roadrunner sheets. That kills just about any thought of sex."

Christina couldn't help laughing. Then she called herself to order and whispered in a seductive tone, "As long as I can look at you and touch you, the sheets don't matter."

The rustling of a bag of chips filtered through the phone. Linda asked, "Are you gay, Chantal?"

"Do you want me to be?"

"Since I have never slept with a woman, I think it would be cool if you were a lesbian. But I hope not all lesbians flirt as aggressively as you do, or I'd be a little paranoid when I work with lesbian patients."

Christina clenched her teeth. This obviously straight woman was making fun of her. "What do you want, Linda?"

"Oh, hi, Christina. What happened to Chantal?"

Christina's pulse raced, and she caught herself snorting into the phone like an angry bull. If this call hadn't brought her so much money, she would have hung up a long time ago. "Linda, either we have phone sex now, or I'm hanging up. I make good money with this job, but not enough to let myself be treated like this."

Linda didn't say anything.

Did she hang up?

"I'm a lesbian, you know?"

Christina's brows shot up. *What?* "But you just said that ..."

"... that I have never slept with a woman. I haven't slept with a man either." After pausing, she added, "Believe me, I'm a lesbian."

What kind of sick joke was this? Linda was twenty-nine. No one was still a virgin at that age. Right? "Is that a joke?" *Damn, I used my normal voice again.*

"No. Chantal?"

"Yeah?"

"Are you a lesbian?"

Obviously, the question wasn't meant for Chantal. "Yes."

Linda didn't answer.

Damn, why can't I keep my mouth shut? It's none of her business.

"I have one more personal question, and then I promise to stop asking questions about you. Okay?"

Christina took a deep breath, then exhaled slowly. "Depends on the question."

"How old are you?"

"Thirty-one."

"Thank you."

Christina said nothing.

"Okay, Chantal, then let's get started with your act."

"Oh yeah, you really know how to seduce a woman."

"Who knew I had such skills? But seriously, what happens afterward?"

Blinking, Christina asked, "What do you mean?"

"Does everyone just hang up after they ... um ... after they come?"

"Most of them."

"And the ones who don't?"

"Either they want another go, or they make small talk for a minute."

"Okay, another go is out, since we skipped the first time," Linda said. "And I'm not in the mood for small talk. Do you have a plan B?"

"We could take care of that first time."

Linda giggled.

That sounds cute. "I've got a question," Christina said.

"Shoot."

"Why don't you want phone sex?"

"The truth?"

Christina shrugged. "What else?"

"I'd love to have phone sex. I never tried it, but I think it would be interesting."

"But?"

"I don't want to do it with an illusion. I want to try it with a woman. A real woman, if you know what I mean."

"I'm sorry," Christina said. "But I can't give you that."

"I know." Linda's words were barely more than a whisper. After a while, she asked, "Would you ever sleep with someone for money?"

Christina blinked. *What's that got to do with anything?* "You mean in real life?"

"Yes"

"No. I wouldn't."

"Not even for one thousand euros?"

"No."

"For five thousand?"

Christina laughed. "No one would be stupid enough to pay five thousand euros for me."

"And if they would?"

Christina thought about it for a while before she asked, "Man or woman?"

"Woman. And good-looking."

Mmhh. "I would do it for ten thousand."

"Ten thousand euros?"

"Yes."

"And for eight thousand?"

Christina shook her head. What a silly conversation. But somehow, this absurd haggling was fun. "Once?"

"The whole night."

"Would she be good in bed?"

"Don't know."

Christina laughed. The joke had gone far enough now. "You wouldn't really spend eight thousand euros for a night with me without even seeing me beforehand, would you?"

"The truth?"

"Yes."

"Yes, I would."

Christina's laughter faded away. *Is she serious?* "You're crazy."

"And you'll earn eight thousand euros if you do it."

"No."

"What do you mean, no?"

"No, I won't do it."

"But you just said you would."

Christina rolled her eyes. She couldn't be serious. "I was joking."

Silence.

"If you do it, I'll give you the money."

"Why?"

"What do you mean?"

"Why pay me so much money for sex? Maybe I weigh a ton and am ugly as sin."

"I hope not."

"But what if I am?"

"Then that's the way it is. But at least I would sleep with a real woman."

"Baby, you can have that for less money. For one hundred bucks you can have some fun with every whore around. At least with every whore who does it with women."

"It would just be an illusion."

And with me it wouldn't? Why doesn't she just get a girlfriend? "What about a one-night stand you pick up at a gay bar?"

"Maybe I'm ugly as sin?"

Christina chuckled. "I don't think so."

"Oh, why not?"

"You said you're good-looking."

"So you paid attention. But that can mean anything."

"What's the real reason, Linda?"

"I want to know beforehand what to expect. I don't want to talk a woman into coming home with me. Who knows how often she goes home with other women."

This whole thing was becoming weirder by the second. Linda had no way of knowing how many women she had gone home with either. "Are you talking about STDs?"

"No, but now that you mention it ... Do you have any?"

"No. How about you?"

"Very funny, Christina."

"Oh, sorry. I forgot."

"Will you do it?"

Silence spread between them.

Eight thousand euros. Eight thousand! She could finally pay the bill for the heating costs; rent for the next few months would be covered, and she could even buy herself a laptop. *Ha, I could even take a vacation and still have some money left over for emergencies.* "Are we talking about normal sex? No fetishes or kinky stuff?"

"Just a harmless first time ... and maybe a second and a third time. Depending on how well things go."

Christina's heart pounded. "Okay."

"Really?"

"Yes." Her voice trembled. *I can't believe it. I'll ...*

"Great." Linda cleared her throat. "Here are the conditions: We'll both get tested for STDs. I'll pay for it. I'll also get tested so you can see that I'm clean. Then you'll come over to my place early one evening and we'll go out to dinner. Any preferences?"

"No." Christina felt like throwing up.

"Okay. I'll pick something. After dinner, we'll go back to my place. Then we'll ... you know what."

Christina swallowed. "Have sex."

A long exhale vibrated through the phone. "Yes. And I want you to stay until the next afternoon. Then you'll get the money."

"How can I be sure that I'll really get the money?"

"Any suggestions?"

"I don't know."

"How about I give you three thousand euros in advance and five thousand afterwards?"

"Okay." She probably would have done it even for

three thousand. She needed the damn money.

"Where do you live?"

"What?"

"In which city do you live?"

"In Cologne. And you, Linda?"

"Berlin."

"When do you want to do it?" Christina flinched. She hadn't wanted to say it like that.

"In two weeks?" Linda didn't seem to notice the ambiguity of her question.

Christina peeked at the calendar on her wall. Except for a math test in three weeks, nothing else was scheduled for this month. "Okay. But you'll have to give me some money for gas."

"No money for gas, but I'll need your bank account to send you the money for the checkup and the plane ticket."

"Plane ticket?"

"Sure. You don't need to take the train or car. A plane will get you here in just one hour."

"But then you'll need my full name."

"Christina, I'm not a crazy stalker. But I can deposit the money with a lawyer of your choice if you want."

"A lawyer?"

"Sure. An intermediary. That way, neither of us needs to know the other's last name."

"All right."

"If I call this number tomorrow evening, will the call go to you again?"

"I'll give you the number for my regular customers. The price is the same, but you'll be put through to me directly."

"At what time should I call?"

"Seven would be good."

"I'm with a patient at seven."

That late? Boy, she's really a workaholic. "What time works for you?"

"Eight?"

"Okay."

"Christina?"

"Yes?"

After a short silence, Linda asked, "Are you really fat and ugly?"

Christina laughed. "No."

Her breath crackled through the phone as Linda exhaled.

Christina laughed again.

"You have a nice laugh," Linda said. "I like it when you laugh."

What am I supposed to say to that? Christina said nothing.

"Sleep well, Christina. Oh, and try some hot milk with honey."

"For what?"

"Your insomnia."

"How did y—?"

"Just a hunch. Good night."

"Good night." Christina ended the call and stared off into space. She would get paid for sleeping with a stranger. Her stomach revolted. But she needed the money. She had no idea what would happen after the second reminder for the heating bill, but she didn't want to find out. Christina plopped down onto the bed. She prayed that Linda hadn't lied to her. She hoped Linda was serious about their deal and that she really wasn't that unattractive.

* * *

Linda peeked through one of the windows in her third-floor apartment and watched the well-lit street. The taxi would be there any second.

Two weeks had passed since she had hired Christina from the sex hotline for tonight. *I can't believe I'll have sex tonight. With a perfect stranger. But that's how I wanted it.* Who cared about the money? But what if she couldn't go through with it or made a fool of herself? What if Christina changed her mind? And what if ...?

A taxi stopped in front of Linda's apartment building.

Oh God, there she is. I can't do this. Should I cancel? Nonsense. Linda looked away. She didn't dare look out the window to see what Christina looked like. When the doorbell rang, she hurried to the door to open it.

A few seconds later, she watched through the peephole as the light went on in the staircase. Footfalls approached.

One last time, Linda glanced at her reflection in the large mirror next to the door. With trembling fingers, she brushed a strand of hair behind her ear. Her hair was just long enough for that. Would Christina like her blue eyes? *Maybe I shouldn't have put on the blue cocktail dress.* Its neckline plunged too deep, didn't it? And the blue high heels ... *Oh God, she'll think I'm one of those superficial chicks with no brains.*

The footfalls in the staircase moved past and then faded.

"Damn," Linda said.

Apparently, Christina had gone past her apartment up to the fourth floor.

Linda took a deep breath and jerked open the door. At the same time, the light went out. She pressed the switch, and the light flared on. "Um, down here," Linda called.

Footfalls came toward her. Christina climbed down the stairs, but as their gazes met, she stopped.

"Christina?"

A slow nod answered her.

They stared at each other without moving. Christina looked incredible. Perfect body, shoulder-length blond hair, and a beautiful face robbed Linda of speech. *She looks so ... innocent.* She would have never imagined a woman who earned her money with phone sex could look like this.

With hesitant steps, Christina came closer and stopped three feet away.

Linda was a bit taller, so she had to look down to keep eye contact. *Oh God, I hope she doesn't think I'm looking down on her.*

Christina wore faded jeans and a white tank top. In one hand, she held a black duffel bag. "Hi," she said. Was her voice shaking?

"Hi." Linda stepped back. "Please come in."

Shining green eyes looked back Linda. Then Christina lowered her gaze and entered the apartment.

Linda closed the door with both hands.

Christina paused next to the door and studied Linda from head to toe.

Linda cleared her throat. "The bathroom is the second door to the right. I put your clothing for tonight in there." After looking at Christina again, she asked, "You're a size ten, right?"

Christina nodded and stepped into the bathroom without looking left or right.

* * *

What am I doing here? Christina stared in the large bathroom mirror. The face in front of her seemed to be that of a stranger. She looked at the floor. *Just don't think about it.*

Never in her life would she have imagined that a woman that good-looking would open the door. *Good-looking? Who are you kidding? She's gorgeous.* Slender, with legs that seemed to go on forever, blue eyes, and dark, chin-length hair—Linda looked like a supermodel. And her dress ... No one looked that good in real life. Christina's gaze slid over the hanger that hung on the shower rod. With narrowed eyes, she checked the size tag in the cocktail dress. *Looks more like a size eight.* Christina shook her head. It didn't matter. Too tight or not, usually wild horses couldn't make her wear a dress. Especially not such a small piece of fabric that barely c—

"Um, do you want something to drink?" Linda called through the closed door.

The question wrenched Christina from her thoughts. "Yes, please. Maybe a glass of water." Her mouth was bone-dry.

"Okay, it ... it'll be waiting for you when you come out."

Wow, Linda's voice was trembling. *She's as nervous as I am.* Christina took a deep breath and undressed. Then she slipped into the dress that had probably cost a small fortune.

* * *

After what felt like an eternity, the bathroom door opened. The first thing Linda saw was one of the red high heels. Then Christina appeared in all her splendor. Linda's breath caught. *God, she looks fantastic.*

Christina was wearing the Ralph Lauren dress Linda had bought for her. It ended above her knee and emphasized her gentle curves. Slightly muscular arms and legs made Christina look feminine and athletic at the same time.

Goose bumps trailed down Linda's back. "You look breathtaking," she whispered.

Christina shifted her weight from one foot to the other. She tugged at her tight dress. "Thanks." She threw a quick glance at Linda. "So do you." Christina's voice was barely audible.

They stood facing each other. Neither moved.

Then Linda glanced at the glass of water on the chest of drawers. She reached for it and cursed under her breath when a bit of water splashed over the rim.

Christina took a hesitant step toward her and reached for the glass. Their fingertips touched, and Christina froze in mid-motion.

Heat shot through Linda. She forced a smile and pulled back her hand. "Sorry." When Christina furrowed her brow, she added, "For the spilled water." Linda stared at her shoes. "I'm really nervous." For what felt like an eternity, Linda didn't hear anything but the TV from her next-door-neighbor, Mrs. Riegler.

Then Christina stepped closer and stood just inches away. With her free hand, she gently lifted Linda's chin until their gazes met. "We're both nervous." The corners of her mouth twitched as if she was trying to smile.

Calm down. Everything will go okay. Linda cleared her throat and gave a hint of a smile. "Um, I should clean up this mess." She glanced at the puddle on the floor. "Then we can go." She darted toward the kitchen and called, "I hope you like Italian food." Seconds later, she dashed back into the hall with a cloth. "Do you?"

Christina blinked. "Do I do what?"

Linda crouched down and mopped up the water while peeking up at Christina. *Great legs.* Linda's cheeks burned. She directed her gaze at Christina's face. "Do you like Italian food?"

"Oh, yes. I do." Christina lifted the glass to her lips and emptied it in one big gulp.

"Great." Linda stood, put the cloth on the umbrella stand, and took her purse from the chest of drawers. "Shall we?"

Christina leaned forward and put the glass on the chest of drawers. Her fingers brushed over Linda's arm.

Linda's breath came in a rapid rhythm, and her heart raced. But before she could react in any way, Christina stepped back. Linda's mouth was as dry as the Sahara. *I have to get a drink as soon as we're in the restaurant.* With that thought, she opened the door.

* * *

Christina followed Linda to the black BMW coupé. She didn't know much about cars, but she could tell that the car was expensive.

Instead of opening the door on the driver's side, Linda paused next to Christina.

What is she doing?

Linda pressed a button on her car key, opened the passenger side door, and held it open for Christina.

Wow. No one had ever treated Christina so courte-ously. *And now that someone is doing it, it's the woman who's paying me to sleep with her.* The thought hit Christina like a punch to the stomach. She sank onto the black leather seat.

Linda closed the passenger side door and strode over to the driver's side.

Christina stared at the dashboard. It looked as if it had been polished recently. *Everything about Linda seems so perfect. Great apartment, great car, great looks, great job ... yet she called a sex hotline on her birthday, so she didn't have to be alone.*

When Linda took her place behind the wheel, she was forced to slide her tight dress up a little.

The sight of Linda's shapely legs made Christina lick her lips. When Christina cleared her throat, Linda looked up and met the gaze of dark blue eyes. *Shit. How embarrassing. She caught me ogling her.* Christina directed her gaze toward the windshield. *So what? That's what she wants, isn't it?*

* * *

Did she just stare at my legs? Linda shook her head. *Nonsense.*

Christina's gaze was fixed on the dashboard.

Is she uncomfortable? Linda had never been on a date. Somehow, it had been very different in her imagination. She couldn't say what she had imagined, but not this. *What did you expect? You're paying her to be here.* Linda swallowed. *And to sleep with you.* Linda squeezed her eyes shut. *But first we've got a reservation at the restaurant.* She opened her eyes and started the car. For the next minutes, she focused solely on the Saturday night traffic.

Christina didn't say anything. She seemed almost paralyzed.

"You're right. We're both very nervous, and that's normal," Linda said, breaking the silence. "Just pretend I'm a one-night stand. Forget the money for now." She peeked at Christina, then back at the street. "If you would sleep with a woman like me without her paying you to do it." Linda's voice was lower now. Did Christina find her attractive? What if she had stared at her legs only because she thought it was expected of her? Part of the job.

Christina said nothing.

How could Linda have thought it would be different? Christina wasn't here because she wanted to, but because she was paid to. That was the only reason.

Linda pulled into one of the many empty parking spaces in front of the restaurant. There was enough free parking for all guests, no matter the day or the hour. That's what she liked about this place.

Linda killed the engine. The silence that followed sounded louder than an air hammer in her ears. *Ignore it.* Linda gathered her purse from the backseat and opened the door. Then she got out of the car and energetically closed the door. She hurried around the car but then realized that Christina had opened the passenger side door without any help and was about to get out. Linda offered her hand to help.

Hesitantly, Christina took Linda's hand and pulled herself up. As soon as she was standing, she let go of Linda's hand as if she had been burned.

Is it so awful for her to touch me? Linda pressed the button on her key. A click, followed by a beeping sound, echoed through the night. She turned toward Christina and tried without success to force a smile.

Christina studied her with an intense gaze. Then she reached out her hand and smiled shyly.

Linda stared at the offered hand and finally reached for it. Only now did she realize that Christina's hand was as cold as her own. Linda straightened her shoulders. Hand in hand, they walked toward the restaurant's entrance.

* * *

The glass door offered Christina a good view of the reception area. A waiter in a suit stood in front of a high table, focusing on an open book in front of him.

When Linda opened the door and held it open for her, Christina entered hesitantly. This restaurant definitely wasn't comparable with the Italian place in her neighborhood.

Linda leaned down to the waiter and whispered something in his ear.

He nodded and led them to one of the tables in an out-of-the-way alcove.

I guess that's the table for special guests.

The waiter pulled out a chair and looked at Christina.

She glanced back and forth between the chair and the waiter and finally sank onto the chair. *Wow, great service.*

Before the waiter could hurry over to Linda, she had taken a seat facing Christina.

Both of them accepted menus and studied them thoroughly, as if they contained all the wisdom of the world.

Christina held her breath. She had suspected that the restaurant was expensive, but the cheapest thing that she could find on the menu cost almost twenty euros. The most expensive one was far more than one hundred euros. "D-do you come here often?"

Linda looked up. "Only on special occasions." She regarded Christina. "Don't worry about the prices. I'll pay, of course."

Lowering her gaze, Christina nodded. *She's paying for dinner and for me.* The thought left a stale taste in her mouth.

"Any idea what you'll get?"

Christina managed only a shake of her head.

The waiter reappeared next to their table.

"Can I get a glass of Cabernet Sauvignon, please?" Linda looked back and forth between Christina and the waiter. "No. A glass of Dom Pérignon."

The waiter smiled fleetingly and turned toward Christina. "What can I get you?"

What was the better strategy? Christina tapped her index finger against her thigh. Keeping her wits about her, or hoping that the evening would be more bearable with a little alcohol?

The waiter kept looking at her, his posture ramrod straight as if he had swallowed a broom.

She usually wasn't much of a drinker. The heck with it. "I'll take the same."

"Of course." Without saying another word, the waiter walked away.

Linda laid the menu on the table. "Should we get the fish platter for two? I always wanted to try that one."

Christina closed the menu and laid it on top of Linda's. "If you want to." She wasn't hungry, but she had to eat something. *It's part of the deal.*

When the waiter brought the champagne, Linda

gave him a friendly smile and ordered their food, then returned her attention to Christina. "I'm very glad to have you here tonight." Linda lowered her gaze. "I'm very self-conscious. For one thing because ... because of the situation and for another thing because you don't seem to want it." She took a sip of champagne. "Or am I wrong?"

Is it that obvious? Christina opened her mouth, but nothing came out. What was she supposed to say? That she really didn't want to be here? That she needed the money but didn't want to sleep with a stranger? Not even with this incredibly good-looking woman across from her.

Linda took another sip of champagne and said, "Your silence speaks volumes." Her tone didn't sound annoyed but matter-of-fact. "It's obvious how uncomfortable you are. And I can't imagine that it'll get better as the evening progresses. This can't work like this."

What? Is she rejecting me? Am I not good enough for her?

On the other hand ... she really hadn't acted in a way that Linda could expect for so much money. *To hell with that.* A hot woman was paying her to get laid. Not going along with it would be stupid. Christina stared at her champagne glass, then into Linda's face. She reached for Linda's hand, leaned forward, and pressed a soft kiss to the back of Linda's hand.

Linda watched her with an expressionless face.

When Christina leaned back, their gazes met. "You're a beautiful woman, Linda. I can't promise that I'll be able to eat even one bite, but I'll spend the night with you. And I'm sure we'll have a good time." Now she only had to believe it too, and everything would be fine.

Linda studied her hands. Was she blushing? "So you're not hungry?"

Christina shook her head.

Linda smiled.

What a nice smile.

Casually, Linda lifted her hand.

Out of the corner of her eye, Christina saw the waiter hurry over.

"I can't eat a thing either," Linda said, grinning.

Both laughed. For the first time since they met, the tension lightened.

They finished their champagne, and when the waiter reached the table, Linda said, "We have to go." She took a one-hundred-euro bill from her wallet. "Keep the change."

The waiter furrowed his brown, hesitantly took the money, and moved behind Linda to help her with the chair.

Linda waved him away. "I don't need any help. Thanks." She gestured in Christina's direction.

The man looked back and forth between them and then hurried over to Christina.

She sent Linda another smile. *She's trying to make me feel good.* When Linda stepped past her, Christina offered her hand.

Linda took it. Together, they left the restaurant.

When they reached the parking lot, Christina stopped and let go of her hand.

Linda looked up. "Everything okay?"

Yes, say yes. You made up your mind, so you have to go through with it. Christina straightened. "Sure."

Smiling shyly, Linda touched her back. They continued to the car.

No way back now.

* * *

What did I let myself in for? With trembling hands, Christina smoothed imaginary wrinkles from her short dress.

After a few minutes, Linda broke the silence in the car. "Can I ask you a personal question?"

Christina peeked in her direction and then watched the traffic in front of them. "You can ask, but I can't promise that I'll answer."

Linda took a deep breath. "Are you single?"

Christina looked at her. "Why?"

Shrugging, Linda said, "I imagine it would be hard to explain to your partner that you'll be spending the night with another woman."

It wasn't really any of her business. *What the heck.* "I'm single."

Linda was silent. Then she asked, "Can I ask one last question?"

"If I can also ask one, sure," Christina said, chuckling.

Linda grinned. "Sounds fair."

"So?" Christina turned toward Linda and gripped the seat with one hand. "What's your question?"

They stopped at a red light, and Linda fidgeted in her seat. "Am I your type?" she asked quietly. She glanced at Christina out of the corner of her eye.

Christina stared at Linda. Had she heard correctly? Her gaze wandered over Linda's slender, sexy body. How could this incredible woman still be a virgin at the age of twenty-nine? It wasn't just her good looks.

Her confidence, mixed with a shyness that sometimes shone through, was irresistible. *Is she my type? Hell, yes!* If only they had met under different circumstances. *Bullshit. I wouldn't have dared walk up to a woman like her, much less ...*

"Guess your silence means no."

What?

Linda bit her bottom lip. "It's okay."

"No. No, you ... I don't have a type that I find attractive. Every woman can be interesting." *Every woman can be interesting? What are you prattling on about?* It was ridiculous. Every night, she said things on the phone that would made her blush just months ago. But now that she was talking face-to-face with a hot woman, she couldn't even tell her how attractive and desirable she was.

"That's a nice way to put it." Laughing humorlessly, Linda glanced at Christina and then back at the street in front of them. "You don't have to make excuses. I can understand that you ..."

Christina lifted one hand. "I'm not saying this because you're paying me for tonight: You're an incredibly good-looking woman. I probably won't get a woman like you even close to my bed for the rest of my life." Christina shook her head. "And if circumstances were different and you wanted me to come home with you, I wouldn't hesitate for a second."

Linda blinked. Once, twice. "Thank you."

"It's the truth."

After a few moments, Linda asked, "So what was your question? You said you had one too."

Christina hesitated. Normally, she wouldn't have asked such a question. It was too personal. *Oh, and having sex with her tonight won't be personal?* She gave herself a mental shove. "Why are you still a virgin? I mean ... with your looks, you can't tell me no one was interested."

Linda pulled into the parking lot in front of her house. She killed the engine and turned toward Christina. "I've never been approached by a woman. And men never interested me. At least not that way. When I was in university, a fellow student wanted to date me, but that was it." Linda sighed. "I've never been one to go out. I guess you could say I'm a bookworm and a couch potato."

Christina hadn't imagined bookworms and couch potatoes to look like Linda. These people were ugly and boring. Linda was a lot of things, but certainly not boring. And she was as far from being ugly as Christina was from getting an A in math.

Linda unfastened her seatbelt and got out of the car. As before, she closed the door and sprinted around the car to open the passenger side door for Christina and to help her out.

Christina reached for the offered hand and got out. Their gazes met. Christina swallowed. No, she wasn't boring at all.

Linda continued to hold her hand as they entered the building.

* * *

Linda's heart pounded. She let go of Christina and unlocked the door to her apartment with trembling hands. "Do you want to use the bathroom?" *Was that my voice?* It sounded tinny to her own ears.

Christina nodded and disappeared.

Linda laid her purse on the chest of drawers in the hall and entered the living room on wobbly legs. Was this really happening? Was she really about to have sex? She took in her surroundings. Everything seemed as unfamiliar as the things that would happen tonight. The couch, the bookcase, the large TV that she rarely turned on, the shelf with her countless DVDs, the photo of—

"Are these your parents?"

Linda flinched and whirled around.

Standing directly behind her, Christina looked at her. Obviously, she had studied the photo.

What fascinating color. Linda stared into Christina's green eyes.

"Linda?"

"I'm sorry. What did you just say?"

Christina furrowed her brow. "The photo."

She wrenched her gaze away from Christina and glanced at the photo. Then she nodded.

"I'm sorry about what happened to them." Christina lifted one hand but paused inches from Linda's shoulder instead of touching her. She dropped her hand and cleared her voice. "Um, would you also like to use the bathroom before we …?"

Linda's heart hammered wildly. How could she have forgotten going to the bathroom? She usually wasn't so absent-minded. If there was one thing she could rely on, it was her sharp mind. But this situation was far from normal. "Yes. Yes, I'll go use the bathroom for a second," she said and left the living room with her knees feeling like rubber.

* * *

Christina sank onto the couch. She'd had a lot of dumb ideas in her life, but this ... Maybe distracting herself would help. She had never been in a psychologist's apartment. Christina rolled her eyes. How stupid of her to think that psychologists were different from normal people. *Who's normal?* Christina grunted. *No one I know.*

The living room was spacious, especially compared to her own one-room apartment. The black leather couch was very comfortable. Her Klobo couch from Ikea definitely couldn't keep up with this. A bowl of fruit sat on a coffee table made of pale wood. Her gaze fell onto the large flat-screen TV. Her old tube TV would have hid in shame compared to this miracle of modern technology. How would it feel to watch a movie on the large screen? She stood and walked over to the entertainment center made of the same pale wood as the coffee table. She touched the material with two fingers. No veneer. Real wood.

Next to the entertainment center was a floor-to-ceiling window. Christina stepped up to the glass and pushed the white, half-transparent curtain aside. She glanced at the brightly lit street. A few expensive cars drove by, and every now and then, people passed on the sidewalk. Everything seemed harmless and normal. At least out there. In here, everything seemed to be caught in a bubble far away from reality.

Christina closed her eyes for a moment. What weird thoughts. Surely the glass of wine was to blame. When something rustled behind her, Christina turned.

Linda stood in front of her, smiling wryly.

Christina swallowed. *Showtime.*

* * *

Linda's whole body trembled. It was time. She hoped Christina couldn't see how nervous she was.

They stared at each other.

Does she want me to begin? Linda's heart pounded in her ears. She took another step toward Christina. Now they stood so close that she felt Christina's breath on her face. *What now?*

As if Christina could read her thoughts, she tilted her head and gave Linda a soft kiss on her lips.

Linda's eyelids fluttered shut. Christina's mouth was so incredibly soft and warm. Were Christina's lips trembling or her own?

Much too fast, Christina leaned back and broke the careful contact.

Linda had to smile. It had felt wonderful. She wanted more.

Christina studied her with an intense gaze. Her chest rose and fell in a quick rhythm.

"W…" Linda cleared her throat. "Want to go to the bedroom?"

Christina stared at her as if she hadn't understood one word. Then she nodded. A damp hand reached for Linda's.

Clinging to Christina like a drowning person to a lifeline, Linda crossed the room on wobbly legs. She stumbled through the hall and into the bedroom. Blue satin sheets glowed in the light of the full moon filtering in through the window.

"Is it okay if we leave the light out?" Linda asked quietly. No one had seen her naked since she'd been a child. Besides, what if Christina didn't find her body attractive?

"Of course."

Linda closed the door by leaning her back against it. Her gaze jumped back and forth between Christina and the bed. *It's now or never.* After taking a deep breath, she reached for Christina's hand, and tugged her closer to the bed. She studied Christina's face in the moonlight. It looked tense. Linda bit her bottom lip. *What do I do now?*

Taking several deep breaths, Christina placed her hands on Linda's hips.

Thank God. She's making the first move.

Christina stepped closer until their bodies touched.

Linda's heart thumped against her ribcage. She couldn't breathe. Was that what a panic attack felt like? Christina's body heat radiated through the thin silk dress. How would it be to feel this heat without any clothing between them?

Christina let go of Linda's hips. She took Linda's face between her hands and pulled her down.

Linda's breath caught. Their lips came closer and closer until they touched.

Once again, the contact ended after just a few moments.

If they continued at this pace, Christina would still be fully clothed at sunrise. *I want to see her without the dress.* It was her turn to do something. *Come on.* Determined, Linda took Christina's face between her hands and pressed her lips against Christina's lightly opened mouth.

Christina stood without moving. She seemed to be in a state of shock.

Did she change her mind? Should I stop? Before Linda could decide, Christina wrapped her arms around her. Then Linda felt a warm tongue find its way into her mouth. A moan broke the silence in the bedroom. *Was that me?*

Very gently, almost hesitantly, Christina's warm tongue played with her own. She repeatedly retreated, allowing Linda to set the pace.

Linda's hands wandered down Christina's back. The silk of the cocktail dress felt cold beneath her fingers. Everything felt unfamiliar, and Christina's kisses were so much better than she'd expected. Linda had thought kisses would be wetter and somehow more invasive. But kissing Christina left her with just one thought: she wanted more! So she began to pull down the zipper on Christina's dress.

Interrupting their kiss, Christina stared at Linda with wide eyes.

Should I stop? Linda froze. *Was I too fast?* "No?"

"Yes." Christina swallowed. "Sure."

Linda hesitated. Christina didn't seem to want this. "Are you sure?"

"Very sure," Christina whispered and pulled Linda's head down.

The kiss that followed left Linda weak-kneed.

Christina kissed her as if she wanted to rip her clothes off.

Then Linda felt her zipper sliding down her back. Goose bumps erupted all over her skin.

With feather-light touches, Christina slid her hands along her shoulders. Rustling, Linda's dress fell to the floor.

Still exploring Christina's mouth, Linda awkwardly tugged on Christina's dress until it slid off her body. Her whole body tingled. *More. I want more.* Christina's warm, soft skin felt like satin, and her kisses … The world started spinning around her. She grabbed Christina's shoulders with both hands.

They broke the kiss. "Everything okay?" The words sounded more like a breath.

"I'm a bit dizzy." Linda sucked in a breath.

"Oh. Uh, we better lie down," Christina said. "Would you rather …?"

Linda patted her shoulder. "No, no. I'm okay." She smiled. "But lying down seems like a good idea."

Grinning, Christina pushed her toward the edge of the bed.

Together they slid toward the middle.

Linda was lying on her back, and Christina leaned over her. After a moment's hesitation, she straddled Linda. "What now?" she asked and smiled.

Before Linda could stop herself, she zeroed in on Christina's amble breasts that were covered by a black lace bra. She swallowed and lifted one hand. "Can I maybe …?"

Furrowing her brow, Christina looked back and forth between her breasts and Linda, then reached back. A few seconds later, her bra dropped to the floor.

Linda's mouth fell open.

Christina's pale skin, especially her full breasts, contrasted sharply with the darker area around her erect nipples.

Linda reached out a trembling hand and gently touched one of Christina's breasts. They were slightly bigger than her own. The pale breast with its darker areola felt like silk.

"Cup them," Christina said.

Does she really mean that? Linda looked at Christina's breasts, then into her face.

Her silent question was answered by a nod.

Linda cupped first one breast, then reached out with her free hand to touch the other. She rhythmically massaged the breasts. They were so soft, so warm, so ... incredible. Almost surreal.

Sighing, Christina leaned into her touch. "Yes," she rasped. "Just like that."

Linda watched Christina lick her lips. It was wonderful. Could she really arouse Christina with her touches? Or was Christina just pretending? *Don't think about it. Just don't think about it.* Christina felt so incredibly good. "I want to feel your naked body on mine." The words had left her mouth without conscious thought, but it was exactly what Linda wanted right now.

"Then take off your underwear." Christina rolled off Linda's body and lay on her back. She lifted her hips and slid off her panties.

Linda's mouth went dry. Christina's body was breathtaking. She was slender but had womanly curves that cried out to be touched.

Christina knelt next to Linda. She trailed her index finger from Linda's neck down to her bra-covered breasts.

Goose bumps covered Linda, yet heat shot through her.

When Christina looked up, their gazes met. "Now you," she said hoarsely.

Linda didn't have to be told twice. She straightened, fumbled with the front clasp of her bra until it opened, and slid off the annoying article of clothing with trembling hands. She threw the bra next to the bed and began to take off her panties, but then she stopped and covered her breasts with her hands.

Christina had stared open-mouthed at Linda's breasts. Now she looked up. Their gazes met again. Carefully, she reached for one of Linda's hands. "Don't do that. They're beautiful." After pausing, she added, "You're beautiful." She gently took Linda's hands in hers and leaned forward. Their lips met in a light touch. Christina slid closer until their breasts brushed against each other.

Linda gasped. This was so ... intimate. This warmth. Everything tingled, as if electricity were running through every cell in her body, down to her clit. Linda kissed Christina passionately and pressed their bodies together, pushing Christina backward until she was lying with Linda on top.

Christina's hands wandered down Linda's back and finally reached her panties. Gently yet determinedly, Christina slid the panties down. She rolled around quickly until she was on top.

Linda squeaked. "What are you doing?"

"I've got to get that off somehow," Christina said and glanced at the panties that she was sliding down Linda's legs and throwing next to the bed. She laughed.

Linda covered her neatly trimmed pubic hair with one hand. "What's so funny?"

"We were both wearing cocktail dresses, but no pantyhose."

"I don't usually wear dresses." Linda smiled. "I'm more a pants kind of gal, and when I realized I needed pantyhose, you were already on your way over."

Christina chuckled. "I don't usually wear dresses either. That's why I didn't notice before."

Both laughed. After a while, they grew silent. As if in slow motion, they drew closer and kissed passionately.

Linda's hands slid across the warm, naked body covering hers. When she felt Christina's bottom beneath her hands, she tightened her fingers.

Christina broke the kiss, sighed, and trailed her tongue down Linda's neck.

God, yes! Linda clutched Christina's ass.

Christina moaned. She nibbled Linda's neck, then sucked gently.

It tickled, but Linda's whole body also pulsed in a way that she had never felt before. Each of her wild heartbeats seemed to end in her clit.

After a while, Christina moved away from Linda's neck and kissed first her collarbones, then the valley between her breasts.

Linda let go of Christina's ass cheeks and slid her hands across the slightly sweaty back above her. The damp skin contrasting with her warm fingers felt fantastic. It was pure eroticism. She never wanted to let go of Christina.

Christina circled Linda's areola with her tongue, moving closer and closer, until her tongue casually flickered across it. She took the nipple into her mouth.

Linda gasped. Her hips lifted instinctively. "Don't stop. Please, don't ever stop."

Despite Linda's pleading, Christina's lips let go after a while and moved toward the other breast. Christina took Linda's nipple into her mouth and suckled enthusiastically.

"Oh, God." Linda pulled Christina's head closer.

Christina sucked a little harder while she stroked the other breast.

Much too soon for Linda's taste, Christina let go of her breast and kissed her way down. She covered Linda's belly with soft kisses, licked and sucked.

What is she planning? She's not going to ...? Linda's breathing picked up until she was almost hyperventilating when she felt a strand of Christina's hair tickle the insides of her thighs.

Christina placed warm kisses on the insides of Linda's thighs.

Gently, Linda caressed Christina's hair.

It happened slowly yet fast at the same time: Christina swiped her warm tongue from Linda's vagina up to her clit.

Linda's breathing came in short bursts. Christina's tongue and what it did became the center of her universe.

Carefully, Christina licked and sucked Linda's clit.

"Oh, oh, yes!" Linda's breath caught.

After a while, Christina looked up. "You have to breathe," she whispered.

Linda exhaled sharply. She began to pant. Air. There just wasn't enough air.

Christina grinned.

Is she laughing at me? Linda's thoughts evaporated when Christina started stimulating the bundle of nerves with her tongue and her mouth again. Never had Linda thought that it would be so wonderful. Her body tingled, and a tension started between her legs, making it impossible to think clearly. Linda glanced down her body.

Christina's head moved in rhythmic circles. When she looked up, their gazes met. Christina's eyes shone. "More?" she asked without letting go of Linda.

"More?"

"Mmhh."

She couldn't think clearly. What was Christina talking about? "Okay," she rasped.

With one finger, Christina stroked toward Linda's opening and circled it.

"Please." Linda was unable to say more. She would have probably done anything to feel Christina's finger inside.

One second later, Christina slid one finger into her.

Linda moaned loudly. Deeper. She wanted to feel Christina deeper. When Christina pulled back her finger, Linda wanted to protest, but then Christina entered her deeply with two fingers.

Christina began a slow rhythm. Her fingers moved in and out, in and out.

Linda's body was ablaze.

Christina's tongue flicked over her clit while her fingers pumped deep inside of Linda.

"God, yes!" Linda started to shake. Her hips moved up and down uncontrollably until her body froze. Her eyelids fell closed. Nothing existed anymore but this incredible feeling. Every muscle in her body tensed.

Quickly, but carefully, Christina moved her fingers in Linda.

Linda's world exploded, leaving behind a wave of heat that flowed through her whole body. Panting, she lay with her eyes closed. It had happened. It had really happened. How long had Christina touched her? Linda had lost all sense of time as her body took over.

Christina held her fingers still inside Linda. She pressed one last kiss to Linda's clit and gently pulled her fingers out.

Everything was sensitive, so Linda was grateful for Christina's gentleness. Her body felt as if it were made of lead. *My God. What was that? I'll never be able to move again.* When something rustled next to her, Linda opened her eyes and saw Christina take two tissues from the box on the nightstand and wipe her mouth and fingers.

Linda's cheeks burned. Christina was wiping off her bodily fluids.

Carelessly, Christina threw the damp tissues next to the bed, slid up toward Linda, and smiled at her.

Linda wanted to return the smile and realized she was already grinning.

Christina laid her hand on Linda's belly, then slid one leg across her thighs.

Linda wrapped her arms around Christina and sighed. This closeness felt heavenly.

Christina placed a soft kiss on Linda's cheek and then laid her head on Linda's shoulder.

"Thank you," Linda whispered before her eyes fell closed.

* * *

Christina blinked. She was lying alone in an unfamiliar bed. The room lay in darkness. Rain drummed against the window. Where was she? What had happened?

She moaned quietly. Linda. She was at Linda's. After having sex, Christina had lain in Linda's arms for a few more minutes while Linda slept. How could she have fallen asleep too? *Because it felt good to lie in her arms.* Everything that had happened in the past hours had felt good. Incredibly good. She looked out the window. Rain had started to fall, but her mood didn't match the bleak weather outside.

Christina had expected to feel dirty or used, and now

that she thought about it, it felt like nothing before in her life. *But do I feel ... like a whore?*

She had enjoyed being intimate with Linda. Feeling Linda react to her touches had been incredibly arousing, and she almost came just watching Linda. The thought made the pulsing between her legs start again.

"Hey."

Christina glanced toward the door.

Clad in a white robe, Linda stood in the doorway and smiled crookedly.

"Hey." Christina pulled the covers up to her neck.

"It's close to midnight, but I thought you might be hungry."

She stared at Linda. *Hungry?*

"I ordered pizza. Since I didn't know what you like, I ordered a Margherita."

Margherita?

Linda regarded her and nibbled on her bottom lip. Finally, she darted past the bed and stopped in front of a large closet. She opened it and rummaged through it for a while. She probably couldn't see a thing because the room was almost dark. Only a little bit of light filtered in from the hall. "Ha!" Linda pulled something out of the closet and carried it to the bed. "I've got a second robe." She studied her feet. "Maybe you'd like to put it on."

Christina gaped at her but didn't take the robe. What else was she supposed to do? This was all so surreal. First she had sex with a stranger, and now this stranger offered her a robe and pizza. If someone had told her a story like that, she wouldn't have believed it.

Linda gave a huge grin. She stood rooted to the spot and frantically played with her fingers. Then she nodded, whirled around, and rushed out of the room as if the devil himself was chasing her. "I'll wait in the living room so you can ... um ... get dressed."

Christina shook her head. *Linda is really strange. But somehow, she's cute too.* She reached for the robe and put it on. *Better than being naked.* She stood and tied the belt of the robe. A pair of slippers stood in front of the bed. Christina put them on. They were a little too big, but soft and comfortable. Slowly, Christina walked toward the open door. The light in the hall hurt her eyes, but she adjusted within seconds.

"Over here," Linda called, and Christina followed her voice to the end of the hall.

Linda stood in the middle of the living room, a large pizza box on a blanket on the floor in front of her. "I thought we could watch a movie."

Furrowing her brow, Christina asked, "How did you know I was awake?"

Linda blushed but didn't look up. "I watched you." She cleared her throat and glanced at Christina. "The pizza was delivered an hour ago. At first, I was worried about the doorbell waking you, but you apparently didn't hear it. Um, I kept it warm in the oven. The pizza, I mean."

Christina swallowed. "You were watching me?"

Linda looked around the room before she met Christina's gaze with wide eyes. "You looked so peaceful. After I woke up, I just couldn't help but ..."

Christina wanted to say, "It's okay." But it wasn't okay. Not at all. When she was awake, she had complete control over her actions and could decide what was allowed and what wasn't. But when she was asleep ... On the other hand, Linda had paid her to sleep with her. *I'm overreacting.* It didn't make sense, but she couldn't shake the feeling that her privacy had been violated. "You couldn't help but what?"

Studying the pizza next to her, Linda murmured, "I couldn't help admiring your beauty."

Christina stared at her through narrowed eyes.

Linda swallowed. She didn't look up and kept her hands folded.

She's being serious. Never before had someone told Christina such a nice thing. At least not without an ulterior motive. But there was no logical reason for Linda to compliment her unless she really meant it.

It was quiet in the room for a while.

"It's okay," Christina finally said. "Um, you wanted to watch a movie?"

Linda glanced up. "If you'd like to." She untied her fingers and lifted both hands. "But we don't have to. I just thought it might be nice."

"Can I take a look at what you've got to offer?" *Oops, I already did.* Heat shot through Christina.

Linda didn't seem to notice the double entendre. She smiled fleetingly and nodded. "Take a look at the shelves. You can pick anything you want. I'll get us something to drink. Any wishes?"

"Coke, if you have it."

"Coming right up," Linda said and hurried to the adjoining room.

Christina watched her retreating back and then stared open-mouthed at large the DVD collection. There had to be more than one hundred movies, maybe even two hundred. *Wow, that's a huge collection.* She read some of the titles. Linda had everything from *Avatar* to *Life of Brian*.

"Did you find something?"

Christina turned. "Nope."

Linda placed two coasters and two glasses of coke on the hardwood floor next to the blanket. Then she walked over to Christina and stopped directly next to her.

Instinctively, Christina took one step to the side. Linda's proximity wasn't uncomfortable, but it somehow seemed ... inappropriate. *Inappropriate? Bullshit. A few hours ago, you had your face between her legs.* Christina shook her head. *Stop thinking.*

Side by side, they looked at the DVD collection.

"There are so many," Christina said.

"I like watching movies." Linda studied her hands. "Watching movies and reading are hobbies that you can do on your own."

Linda's words hit Christina like a blow to the solar plexus. Never before had she met someone as lonely as Linda. Gently, she touched Linda's forearm. "You pick."

Linda looked into her eyes for a long time. Then she glanced at her mouth.

Does she want to kiss me?

But Linda didn't. She turned back toward the shelf and looked at her DVD collection. "There are some I haven't seen yet."

"Really? Why not?"

"The truth?"

Christina smiled. "What else?" When Linda kept silent, Christina nudged her. "Come on. Tell me."

Linda avoided eye contact. "I didn't dare watch them alone."

Huh? "Didn't dare?" *What kind of movies are they? Porn?* "Which one for example?"

"*Final Destination.*"

Christina grinned.

"And *Blair Witch Project*."

For a few moments, she wanted to tell Linda how cute she was. *Don't even think about it. She's paying you to be here, not to compliment her or feed her lines.* It was a job. Nothing else. "Okay, then let's watch one of those movies."

A smile darted across Linda's face before she asked quietly, "*Misery*?"

Christina shrugged. "Sure. Why not?"

"Okay." Linda put the DVD into the DVD player and started the movie.

"Do you want to sit on the couch instead of the blanket?" Christina asked.

Linda looked back and forth between the blanket and the couch. Finally, she nodded. "Whatever you prefer."

Christina reached for the pizza box and sat on the couch.

Linda put the cokes onto the small table next to the couch and sank into the leather that had probably cost a fortune. She tugged her feet beneath her thighs.

There was a yard of empty space between them.

Christina watched Linda carefully. *She's feeling insecure. Is she scared to look like she's coming on to me?* So far, Linda had tried to be as close as possible. That she wasn't doing that now was illogical—or wasn't it? Christina cleared her throat.

Linda abruptly turned her head and looked in her direction.

"Should I ...? Do you want me to move a little closer?"

Linda's cheeks turned bright red. Staring down at her lap, she said quietly, "If you want to."

Cute. Christina moved closer. The robe slid up, and

her naked thigh touched Linda's. Her skin tingled, but Christina didn't move away. She enjoyed watching Linda's blush becoming even darker. *Incredible. Not too long ago, we were rubbing our naked bodies against each other, and now she's blushing at this harmless touch.*

The movie started, and Linda gazed at the TV, totally captivated.

Christina watched her. *Is she really focused solely on the movie? What's going on in that pretty head? Ah, doesn't matter. I'm getting paid to watch movies and eat pizza. Who cares what she's thinking?* Christina knew she was kidding herself. What Linda thought of her did matter. Did she really enjoy the sex? Was she just a prostitute for Linda? *But then she wouldn't have complimented me like that, and she certainly wouldn't treat me like a normal guest. I'm thinking too much.* Christina directed her gaze toward the TV.

They ate lukewarm pizza, and from time to time, Christina leaned across Linda to take a sip of the coke that was sitting on the small table next to the couch. Christina had to repeatedly bite back a smile because every time she leaned forward, Linda turned her attention to her chest, then quickly returned it to the TV. Somehow, it turned Christina on that Linda seemed to find her body attractive.

The empty pizza box landed on the floor.

"May I ... may I ... um ... cuddle up to you?"

How could I say no? God, she's cute. "Of course," Christina said.

Hesitantly, Linda moved closer and leaned her head against Christina's shoulder.

Christina wrapped one arm around Linda's shoulders

and pulled her closer. "Comfortable?" she asked quietly.

"Mhm."

Christina smiled and turned back toward the movie.

A few minutes later, Linda flinched. The male main character in the movie just had his legs broken, and Linda hid her face against Christina's neck. "Oh, God."

Christina chuckled.

"That's not funny," Linda mumbled, still burrowing her face against Christina's neck.

"Yes, it is."

"No."

"Yes."

"Noooo."

"Yes. And now watch the movie."

"Is the bad scene over?" Linda's words were barely comprehensible, but they tickled Christina's neck.

"Yes. You can look again."

Hesitantly, Linda lifted her head. "He's never going to make it out alive," she shouted. "She's completely nuts."

Christina burst out laughing. "Completely nuts? What kind of psychologist are you? Is that your professional diagnosis?"

Now both of them were laughing.

When Linda calmed down, she said, "Looks like a schizoaffective disorder. And I'd say borderline." Linda took a sip of coke and waved her hand. "But I'd need more diagnostic data to be sure."

Huh? Christina stared at her.

Linda rolled her eyes. "Short version: she's completely nuts. Want some ice-cream?"

"Ice-cream?" *How did she come up with that idea?*

"Yes. Ice cream. Vanilla or cherry?"

"Uh, both?"

"You got it." Linda stood and ambled toward the kitchen.

* * *

As soon as the kitchen door closed behind Linda, she leaned her back against it. *If only I knew what to say to her.* Whenever Linda relaxed a little, she said something stupid. Christina probably thought she was totally gaga. How could she use all that technical jargon? Linda groaned. And her "completely nuts" explanation hadn't been a highlight either. *Does she realize how insecure I feel?*

Christina seemed so confident, so cool.

She, however, was awkward all the time. Christina probably thought she was childish for getting so involved in the movie. Adults didn't do that. Linda shuffled to the cupboard and got two small bowls, then she took two spoons and an ice-cream scoop from the drawer. She opened the freezer and shook herself as the cold penetrated the material of her robe. Quickly, she reached for the ice cream and closed the freezer. She paused. The shivers running down her spine ... Her body was more sensitive than usual. Incredible what kind of effect Christina had on her.

Linda closed her eyes. Christina's touches had felt wonderful. If she had known how wonderful sex could be, she wouldn't have stayed a virgin for so long. That was for sure. But that feeling paled in comparison to the comfort she felt holding Christina in her arms. Linda opened her eyes. Time was flying. *Tomorrow, she'll be gone.* Why did the thought hurt so much? She didn't even know Christina.

Brooding would do her no good. For now, Christina was still here, and she would make good use of the time remaining. She straightened and prepared their bowls of ice cream.

* * *

When Linda returned from the kitchen and handed her a bowl of ice cream, Christina said, "I stopped the movie."

"Thanks. That's nice of you." Linda sat next to her and regarded her bowl and its contents.

"Want me to rewind? Should be about three minutes."

"No, that's okay," Linda mumbled, her mouth full of ice cream. "Did I miss anything important?"

"Not really. He's trying to finish the book. Oh, and he's not taking his medication. He's hiding the pills."

Linda nodded and pressed "play." Captivated, she watched the events in the movie and set a new record in emptying her bowl.

Does she always eat that fast? Probably not, or she wouldn't have this killer body. Christina couldn't finish her ice cream. She leaned across Linda to put her bowl on the table next to her. Their gazes met.

Linda licked her lips.

As if in slow motion, their faces came closer and closer until ... dramatically loud music made them look at the TV.

The movie's main character was trying to escape from his prison.

Leaning back, Christina watched.

"Oh God, oh God. She'll get him." Linda squeaked.

"She'll kill him. Oh God." She covered her face with one hand.

Christina regarded the woman next to her. She was much more entertaining than the movie. She smiled. One moment, Linda was totally serious, the next, she was almost childlike.

When the movie's dramatic music gave way to quieter sounds, Linda turned her head but kept her gaze on Christina's knees. "I'm sorry. You probably think I'm totally ..."

"What?" Christina lifted her hand and softly stroked Linda's cheek. "That you're totally cute?" She smiled. "Absolutely." The last word was just a whisper. She put her hand on the nape of Linda's neck and carefully pulled her toward her.

Their faces moved closer until their lips met.

When they broke the kiss after just a few seconds, Linda blinked repeatedly.

Instead of kissing her again, Christina hugged Linda. She couldn't help herself. *What the hell is going on with you? Are you getting sentimental now? Oh, who cares?* Linda felt good. Everything else wasn't important. Christina's eyelids fluttered shut.

Linda held her tightly. "Is everything okay?" she asked quietly.

Hesitantly, Christina nodded. *No, nothing is okay.* She was so confused.

Some time later, Linda let go of her and turned off the TV. She stood, reached for Christina's hand, and led her through the hall and into the bedroom.

To hell with the end of the movie.

* * *

Linda's thoughts were racing. If only she could grasp one of them. Directly before they had kissed in the living room, she had thought she'd seen insecurity and something like fear in Christina's eyes. And the kiss ... it had been so gentle. Why had Christina kissed her? And why had she interrupted their kiss to hold her? She pulled Christina after her and stopped in front of the bed, where she let go of her hand and lay down in the middle of the bed.

For a few seconds, Christina stared at her.

Or is she looking through me?

Christina's expression was unreadable.

Linda sat and reached for Christina. She didn't know why she'd led her to the bedroom and wanted to hold her now. It just felt right. "Come here," she said quietly.

Christina swallowed and crawled onto the bed.

Linda pulled her toward her.

Instead of cuddling against her, completely relaxed, Christina's body now felt a little tense. Christina's head rested against her shoulder, and after a moment's hesitation, Linda combed her fingers through Christina's hair.

A thought hit her like a blow: *She's ashamed of what she has done.* Linda's breath caught, and she stopped in mid-motion. What should she do now? Did Christina experience her closeness as something terrible? No. If that were the case, she wouldn't have hugged her. Unless ... maybe she'd done that just so she didn't have to continue kissing her. *Nonsense. She kissed me, not the other way around. See?* She continued to draw circles through Christina's hair. Or had she done that just because she thought it was expected of her? *Maybe tensing up because she thinks I want to sleep with her again.* "Is it very awful for you?" Linda asked. It was hardly more than a whisper.

Silence.

"Christina?"

Even breathing was her only response. Christina had fallen asleep.

* * *

Warmth. Comfort. Everything felt right. A heart beat evenly, keeping a slow rhythm. Boom. Boom. Boom. *Wait a minute. Whose heart?* Christina opened her eyes wide. A pair of breasts. She lifted her head and studied Linda's face that appeared young and vulnerable in the moonlight.

Linda opened her eyes, and her gaze zeroed in on Christina. "Hi."

She's awake? Christina rolled to the side. "Hi."

"You fell back asleep."

Christina looked at her hands. "I'm sorry."

Linda sat up, straightened her robe, and slid until her back touched the bed's headboard, interrupting bodily contact with Christina. "You don't have to apologize." She stared at her hands that she had folded on her lap. "I am the one who has to apologize."

One of Christina's eyebrows lifted. "What are you talking about?"

"This is awful for you." She looked at Christina with sad eyes. "Isn't it?"

The meaning of Linda's words was clear. But what should she say? Was it awful for her to lie in bed with Linda? No. Did she feel awful now that she had slept with Linda? *Amazingly, no.* What was going on with her? She had slept with a stranger for money. Goddammit, why didn't she feel exploited, dirty, or at least sad? *Did I become so blunted because of that stupid phone job?*

"Nothing further is going to happen between us," Linda said. It didn't sound cold but rather sad. "It wasn't your own free will to ..."

Christina sat up abruptly. "That's not true. It was my free will."

Linda gazed at the floor. "It didn't happen against your will, but if circumstances were different, you wouldn't have done it." She explored Christina's face with an intense gaze. "Would you?"

Was she right? Christina had never had a one-night stand before. After four relationships, two of them long-term, she definitely wasn't a prude anymore. But meeting a woman and having sex with her on the same day ... she normally wouldn't have done that. "You're right." Linda opened her mouth, but Christina added, "But not for the reason you think."

Linda tilted her head. "What do you mean?"

"I normally don't have sex with strangers." She shrugged. "Call me old-fashioned, but I want to be intimate with a woman because I like her and find her attractive." She paused and then added, "And I'm not just talking about physical things."

Linda studied Christina's face. After a few moments that seemed endless, she asked, "If you could travel back in time, would you accept the offer I made you two weeks ago?"

Gheez, what a question. Would she? Linda hadn't treated her badly at any time. Quite the opposite. She was friendly, polite, and had a great sense of humor. Christina couldn't think of one negative thing about

Linda. So with everything she now knew, would she still accept the offer? "Yes." *Without a doubt.* "It's wonderful with you."

A smile darted across Linda's face.

"And you?" Christina asked. "Would you make the offer again?"

"Yes," Linda said. After a pause, she added quietly, "I also think it's wonderful with you."

Christina watched her intently. Why couldn't they have met under different circumstances? "What would you like to do now?"

Linda tilted her head. "What do I want to do now?"

"Yes." They had talked enough. *Jesus, I had relationships where I didn't talk as much about my feelings as I did tonight.*

After a long silence, Linda said, "I would like to take a hot shower and then give you a massage." She lowered her gaze before she looked at Christina, her expression tense. "Only if that's okay with you, of course."

Christina furrowed her brow. "You want to give me a massage?"

"Yes."

"Oh, and where?"

"Wherever you want. Um, if you want."

Did she want it? Her last massage had been so long ago that she couldn't even remember it. "Okay," Christina said. "I'll shower after you and then you can give me a massage."

Linda grinned from ear to ear. "Let's do it that way." She jumped up and rushed toward the bathroom. When she reached the door, she stopped and turned around, smiling. "I'll put towels out for you when I'm done."

"Thanks."

Linda closed the bathroom door behind her.

Christina shook her head. It was crazy. Really crazy. But she couldn't think of a place where she would rather be right now.

* * *

Christina stopped in front of the bed. She was now seeing it for the first time with the lights on. She ran one hand through her towel-dried hair.

"Lie down on your belly," Linda said and slid more toward the edge of the bed.

Christina tugged at her robe. "Should I take this off?"

Linda smiled. "That would make it easier."

Don't be so shy. You'd think you're the virgin. Christina glanced at the tied belt of her robe. Her cheeks burned. *She has already seen you naked.* Awkwardly, she fumbled with the knot until it opened, then she slid off the robe.

Linda had kept her gaze on Christina's face, but as the robe fell to the floor, her gaze flickered to her breasts and then her genital area.

Christina cleared her throat.

Quickly, Linda looked up.

How cute. She's blushing. Christina climbed onto the bed and lay down on her belly. At first, nothing happened. Then she felt Linda straddling her.

Linda gasped.

Apparently, Linda had forgotten that she wasn't wearing anything beneath the robe. Christina grinned. Linda's pubic hair gently tickled Christina's back.

Neither of them said or did anything.

After a while, Christina felt warm hands caress her

back. It was a tentative exploration, not a massage. Christina moaned low in her throat. It felt heavenly. The touches became more determined.

Linda's fingers skillfully kneaded the muscles in Christina's shoulders and neck.

"Oh, that feels divine," Christina murmured. "Where did you learn how to do that?"

"My mother often had tense muscles, so I sometimes gave her a massage."

Christina could hardly focus on the conversation. But she was curious. "What did your father do for a living?"

"He was a lawyer."

"Mmhh."

"What does 'mmhh' mean?"

Christina opened her eyes and only then realized that her eyes had fallen closed. "What?"

"Nothing." Linda laughed. "You don't often get a massage, do you?"

"No." The word sounded like a moan.

Linda's clever fingers kneaded Christina's tense neck muscles.

"Ah, don't stop."

Linda giggled. "What are you offering as a payment?"

"What do you want?" Christina smiled.

Silence.

After what felt like an eternity, Linda said, "Tell me something about you."

"About me?" Christina turned her head until she could see Linda out of the corner of her eye.

Linda's massage stopped.

Their gazes met. Talking about herself was the last thing Christina wanted right now. She had rarely talked about herself with her partners, so why should she do it with Linda? *How do I get out of this without rejecting her?* Christina turned her head away.

Tenderly, Linda trailed her fingertips across Christina's back.

Goose bumps covered every inch of Christina's body.

"I know you're incredibly attractive and that you get this little dimple between your eyebrows when you're insecure or annoyed," Linda said. "I know your dress size and your shoe size. Mmhh … when you're nervous, you can't eat. And I know that you work for a sex hotline. Oh, and you're single and gay of course."

Abruptly, Christina turned onto her back. She held on to Linda's waist so that she wouldn't fall off.

Linda chuckled, but then her expression sobered.

Christina's eyes explored Linda's half-open robe, the neatly trimmed hair between her spread legs, the flat belly, and the partially covered breasts. She had to swallow. Linda's hips beneath her hands felt warm. Should she let go? *Hell, no!*

Linda stared too.

Following her gaze, Christina almost laughed. *We're staring at each other's breasts like two adolescent boys.* But unlike a teenager, she knew what to do to have a good time. And that's what she would do now. While Christina's hands wandered beneath Linda's robe and reached for her hips, she looked into her eyes.

Without ending their eye contact, Linda opened her robe. First she slid it off one shoulder, then the other. Slowly, Linda leaned forward and gently stroked Christina's breasts. "It's wonderful with you," Linda whispered before her lips covered Christina's.

It was like a warm blanket covering Christina.

Linda's touches felt as right as nothing before in her life.

Linda's tongue entered Christina's mouth and made her moan.

Carefully, Christina caressed Linda's back until she grasped two muscular ass cheeks.

Linda sighed into Christina's mouth and deepened the kiss.

Christina was already wet. She wanted Linda.

But Linda ended the kiss and leaned on her hands.

Did I do something wrong?

"May I touch you?"

She stared at Linda. *Did I understand that correctly?* Linda wanted to pleasure her and would even pay her for it? Christina couldn't believe Linda's question. Could Linda touch her? *God, yes!* Christina nodded.

Linda leaned down. Her breasts pressed against Christina's. Soft kisses covered every inch of Christina's face like a cool breeze on a hot summer day. At the same time, Linda caressed the outsides of Christina's thighs.

Christina's pulse sped up. When Linda's mouth covered hers again, Christina invitingly parted her legs to make room for Linda.

Linda moved lower, kissed Christina's left breast, and after a while, she began to suck on her nipple.

"Oh." Intense pulsing started between Christina's legs.

As Christina had done a few hours ago, Linda covered one breast with her right hand while her mouth explored the other.

She's a quick study. "Ah." *Very quick.*

Linda suckled a little harder and then flicked her

tongue across the hardened nipple. "Is that okay?" Linda asked without letting go of the nipple.

"Ah." Christina pressed her closer.

Linda continued to caress Christina's breast with her mouth while she leaned on one arm and slid one hand down. She stroked every rib and every mole she encountered.

Christina's breathing quickened. Linda's tongue and hands were a miracle of nature. She seemed to know exactly what to do to drive Christina out of her mind.

Tenderly, Linda caressed Christina's belly until she reached her pubic hair. But instead of moving lower, she stopped. With a low plop, she let go of Christina's nipple.

Christina opened her eyes and gaped at her.
What? That was it?

Linda's eyes shone with passion, and her cheeks were reddened. "I want to taste you." She licked her lips, emphasizing her words.

Moaning, Christina let her head fall back on the bed. If this was a dream, she never wanted to wake up. "God, yes. Yes, please."

Linda gave her a quick kiss on the mouth.

Next, Christina felt her legs being parted and Linda's lips exploring her belly, her groin, and finally the insides of her thighs. Linda's mouth moved closer and closer to Christina's center.

"Mmhh ... salty," Linda murmured. Almost at the same time, Linda's tongue swept from Christina's open-ing to her clit.

Christina gasped for breath and peeked down for a second. Linda was doing this for the first time? Damn, she was a natural.

Linda had her eyes closed and held on to Christina's legs. She took Christina's clit into her mouth and suckled very carefully while her tongue moved in slow circles around Christina's clit.

Christina's breath came in short gasps. The world around her ceased to exist; she sensed only what Linda did with her. *More, more.* With both hands, she pressed Linda between her legs.

Linda rhythmically moved her tongue back and forth.

"Yes ... yes ... oh, yes." Christina's hips arched uncontrollably. Never before had her body reacted like this. Heat built up in Christina's body, and the only thing she felt was Linda's rhythm. The pulsing in her center spread and seemed to engulf her whole body. "God, I'm coming!" Christina clutched Linda's shoulders.

Linda groaned quietly but said nothing.

Christina exhaled sharply, and her heartbeat slowed. Her firm grip on Linda's shoulders became a gentle embrace. Sluggishly, she lifted her head. "Come up here." Christina's voice was hoarse.

A hint of a smile played around Linda's lips, but it seemed insecure, as if she wanted to know if what she'd done had been okay.

Christina glanced to the side, took a package of tissue from the nightstand, and held them out to Linda. Smiling, she said, "You probably want to clean up a little."

Hesitantly, Linda took two tissues and wiped her mouth, avoiding eye contact. She leaned forward and threw the damp tissues in the trash basket next to the desk. The package of tissues landed on the other side of the bed.

"Come here." Christina felt so close to her.

Carefully, Linda snuggled against Christina.

"Hold me," Christina whispered and hugged Linda.

Linda wrapped one arm and one leg around Christina.

For a while, they just lay there until Christina said quietly, "You're incredible."

Linda propped herself up on one elbow and studied Christina's face. "Incredibly good or incredibly bad?"

Christina's mouth fell open. "Are you kidding?"

"Um, no?"

"Incredibly good." Christina stretched. "Never in my life did I … I've never … You're awesome."

Grinning broadly, Linda said, "Thanks. You too."

Both laughed.

"What now?" Linda asked when their laughter ceased.

"What do you mean? Want to go again?" *Say yes. Please say yes.*

Linda wiggled her eyebrows. "Is that an offer?"

"If the answer is yes, then yes, it is."

"Yes." Linda giggled like a teenager and nodded.

Smiling, Christina pulled Linda down and kissed her passionately. It would be a long night.

* * *

Christina's eyes opened. She blinked in the sunlight filtering in through the window. A glance across the still sleeping Linda to the alarm clock on the nightstand revealed that it was half past eleven. On weekends, Christina liked to sleep late if she'd worked the whole night. But unlike now, she was fully rested then. *When did we finally go to bed?* Go to bed? No, the question was when had they finally fallen asleep. The sun had long since risen when they had stopped out of pure exhaustion.

Linda's hunger for sex, for her, had been insatiable. *Be honest. You couldn't get enough of her either.* Without a doubt, a few of her muscles would complain about their activities last night and this morning. But it had been worth it. She had never had such great ... *What's that?* Was Linda nibbling on her neck? "What are you doing?"

"What does it feel like?" Linda murmured and trailed her tongue down Christina's neck.

Grinning, Christina said, "It feels like you didn't get enough even after last night."

"What if that's the case?" Linda's hands wandered from Christina's shoulders to her breasts. Carefully, she massaged the soft curves.

Christina's eyes fell closed, and she moaned quietly. Linda knew exactly how she wanted to be touched. Still ... Christina opened her eyes wide. "Then I'd say I need to go to the bathroom, but I'm not sure I can walk after last night."

Linda, who was busy exploring one of Christina's breasts with her mouth, lifted her head and grinned. "Now that you mention it, I need to use the bathroom too. How about this: I'll use the bathroom and take a quick shower, and then the bathroom is all yours while I make breakfast. After breakfast, we'll decide what to do with the rest of the day. Okay?"

Christina glanced at Linda, who lay half on top of her. No woman looked so beautiful after a night of wild sex and little sleep. How did Linda do it? Even with tangled hair, she was irresistible. The past hours had been like a dream, and the comfort she experienced in Linda's arms ... Hold on. Comfort? That was ridiculous. After all, Linda was ...

"What are you thinking about?"

"Mmhh?"

"You look so serious," Linda said. "What are you thinking about?"

Should she tell her the truth? *Certainly not.* There was nothing to say. She was thinking nonsense. That was all. *It's probably the lack of sleep.* But one thing was true: "It's wonderful with you."

As if in slow motion, Linda stroked Christina's cheek with the back of her hand. "I think it's wonderful too."

When their gazes met, time seemed to stand still.

Then Christina caressed Linda's back with her fingertips.

Linda closed her eyes. After a few seconds, she opened them and stood. "If I don't get up now, we won't make it out of bed today."

Without Linda's warmth above her, Christina shivered. She pulled the covers up to her neck.

"Any special requests for breakfast?" Linda asked while she was sitting on the edge of the bed and reaching for her robe.

"Toast and orange juice, please."

Linda stood, put on her robe, and tied it. "You're easy to please."

Christina grinned. She had barely slept a wink, yet she couldn't remember a morning when she'd felt as happy. Had she ever been truly happy in her life? Content, sure. Happy ... no. *Stop the brooding. It's a wonderful morning. Enjoy it.* Christina sat up and pecked Linda's lips. "You've got no idea."

* * *

Christina was just climbing out of bed when Linda

left the bathroom. "Why are you blushing?" *Is she ashamed of last night?*

Linda lowered her gaze. Her cheeks took on an even darker hue of red. "My legs are wobbly after last night," she mumbled without looking up.

Oops. Christina tried to keep her expression neutral but failed miserably. She couldn't help giggling and then burst out laughing.

Her face expressionless, Linda stared at her. "That's not funny."

Christina gasped for breath but couldn't stop laughing. Tears formed in her eyes. "Yes, it is."

Linda crossed her arms over her chest. "This is embarrassing enough without you laughing at me."

Was she serious? Christina's laughter stopped. "Um. I'm sorry. I'm not laughing at you. Really."

Linda lifted one brow.

Moaning softly, Christina stood and hauled herself toward Linda, who stood before her in her robe. She, too, had more sore muscles than expected. Linda's gaze on her naked body felt like the tender touches from last night.

But Linda's posture was still stiff.

Christina paused directly in front of her. "Do you seriously think I'm doing any better?"

Linda dropped her arms and shrugged.

"The answer is 'no.' Jesus, I never before had so much sex in so little time. Not that I'm complaining." Christina winked.

Again, Linda blushed.

Christina reached for one of Linda's hands, lifted it to her lips, and kissed it gently.

Linda watched her every movement and leaned

forward. Slowly, she kissed Christina on the mouth and then moved back. "I'll make breakfast."

"Okay." On slightly shaky legs, Christina padded to the bathroom.

* * *

For the umpteenth time, Linda moved Christina's glass of orange juice a little to the left, then a few inches to the right. Everything had to be perfect. As perfect as it could be under these circumstances. Linda examined the fully set table. What was the saltshaker doing here? They didn't have eggs. Shaking her head, she reached for it and stood. She took two pieces of bread and put them into the toaster. Her short nails drummed a beat on the counter. Normally, it didn't take so long for the toast to be done.

Drying her hair with a towel, Christina entered the kitchen.

Linda stopped in mid-motion and stared toward the door.

They looked at each other. Neither moved.

Linda's heart hammered against her rib cage. Her gaze wandered over Christina's body that was covered only by the white robe. *God, she's so sexy.* Her thoughts were interrupted when Christina walked over and sat at the kitchen table. *What was I about to do?* With a click, two pieces of toast jumped at Linda. She caught them and immediately let go when pain shot through her fingers. "Ouch. Damn." One piece of toast was about to fall off the counter. She juggled the toast and finally threw it into the basket in front of Christina. The second piece followed. Linda's cheeks burned as she sat at the table. "Sorry."

Christina smiled but said nothing.

After Christina took a piece of toast from the basket, Linda followed her example and started to butter her toast. Then she added a layer of jam. She took a big bite. If they ate breakfast as if nothing had happened, maybe Christina would forget her clumsiness. But out of the corner of her eye, she saw Christina watching her every movement.

Christina hadn't touched her own breakfast.

After some time, Linda put her toast down and smiled shyly. "What?" Okay, she was a klutz, but that was no reason for staring at her.

Peeking at the glass of jam, Christina asked, "How does passion fruit jam taste?"

Oh. She's interested in the jam, not me. Linda lowered her gaze for a moment. *How could I let myself think that? I should know better.* "You haven't tried it before?"

"Nope."

Linda looked at her half-eaten toast. "Want to try?"

"I'd like that."

Linda held out her piece of toast.

Christina took a bite, looking deeply into Linda's eyes. She almost bit one of Linda's fingers.

"Hey, I need those if we go back to bed later," Linda said, grinning.

"Delicious." Christina chuckled. "Oh, was that an offer?"

Linda's mouth fell open when Christina gave back her playful question from last night. What should she answer? Yes, yes, yes? Hesitantly, she nodded.

Christina plucked the toast from her hand and laid it on the plate in front of her.

What is she doing?

Smiling, Christina took a sip of orange juice and reached for Linda's hand.

"What ...?"

Christina stood and pulled Linda up. Without any warning, she pressed her mouth against Linda's. Her tongue quickly entered Linda's mouth.

Linda moaned softly. Her body knew only one goal: feeling Christina's bare skin against hers. Linda's hands untied the belt of Christina's robe, pushed the robe off her silky shoulders, and slid over every inch of naked skin she could reach. When cool air hit her overheated body, Linda realized that she wasn't wearing her robe anymore. How had Christina ...? "Ahhh." Her ass cheeks were taken in a firm grasp while Christina's tongue explored her neck.

"Let's ... mmhh ... let's go to the bedroom," Christina murmured without interrupting her assault on Linda's neck.

"Okay." Linda gasped and moved backward. Christina's hands seemed to be everywhere, and they felt so incredibly good. When she took one more step back, Linda stumbled over her own feet. One moment later, she lay on the floor on her back with Christina on top of her.

"Oh, God, did you hurt yourself?" Christina propped herself up on both hands and looked at her wide-eyed.

Linda shook her head. "What about you?"

"I'm fine." Christina's dark red tongue slowly licked her lips. "Where were we?"

"We're in the kitchen." Linda giggled.

"So? If I'm not mistaken, you've got floor heating."

"Um, yes. But ..."

Christina's expression sobered. "Take me. Here and now."

Linda lifted both brows. *On the kitchen floor?* But who was she to deny such a request?

* * *

Linda tenderly stroked Christina's back, enjoying the warmth of the body that partially covered hers. Christina's skin was so warm, so ... silky. She sighed quietly. It was so incredibly relaxing. Her gaze wandered aimlessly through the room and fell on the alarm clock on the nightstand. The realization hit her like a blow. Oh, no. "Christina?"

"Mmhh?"

"We've got to get up."

Lazily, one eye opened, then the other. "Why?"

"Your flight is leaving in two hours."

Wide-eyed, Christina stared at her.

Linda pointed at the alarm clock.

Christina stared at the clock without moving. Then she rolled to the side and sat on the edge of the bed. She took a deep breath, stood, and reached for her traveling bag lying in front of the closet. Without turning, she left the room.

Linda's stomach clenched. That was the end of their ... business arrangement.

* * *

Christina closed her eyes as the spray of the shower hit her body and face. It was just a job. Nothing else. What was going on with her? Why did it feel wrong to leave? *The sex was good, okay, but ... Wait a minute! Good? It was great. But still. That's what she paid you for. It was a job. Nothing else.* These sentences became her mantra.

Christina scrubbed her body and washed her hair twice. She didn't feel dirty or used but was still trying to wash away the memories of Linda, the sense of comfort and ease. Not because she wanted it, but because it was the right thing to do. Yes, it was the right thing.

* * *

Straightening her shoulders, Christina left the bathroom. Her hair was still wet. She wore olive-green cargo pants, and a black tank top clung to her still damp skin.

Linda stared at her. *She's breathtaking.* As soon as Christina had disappeared into the bathroom, Linda had hastily dressed. Now she was wearing blue jeans and a white T-shirt. Nothing spectacular, but enough for driving to the airport.

Furrowing her brow, Christina asked, "Why are you dressed?"

"I want to take you to the airport."

"I don't know if that's such a good idea."

The words hit Linda like a blow to the solar plexus. *She's got every right to decide. You're just her ... her client.* "Whatever you want. I'll call you a cab." Linda shuffled to the nightstand, where her wallet was. She took out a one-hundred-euro bill and held it out to Christina.

Christina eyed the money but made no move to take it.

Linda took a half step toward her. "The money is for

the cab."

Glancing back and forth between Linda's face and the money, Christina said, "That's too much."

"Take it. Please. You can tip the cabbie or buy yourself something at the airport."

Christina opened her mouth but said nothing. Instead, she nodded and took the money.

Linda reached for the phone next to the bed and called a cab. She threw the phone on the bed. Together, they walked to the front door. Every step was harder for Linda than the one before. *I don't want this. I don't want this.*

Christina turned toward Linda. Her right hand moved behind Linda's neck and pulled her down.

They exchanged a deep, tender kiss.

Heat flashed through Linda, but she wasn't just aroused. She wanted to hold Christina and never let go, wanted to experience her warmth and her smell just a little bit longer. Saying good-bye hurt almost physically. But still, after a while, they let go, both breathing heavily.

Christina stroked Linda's hot cheek. "Good-bye."

Linda said nothing. She watched Christina open the door and then close it behind her. Linda leaned against the closed door and shut her burning eyes.

* * *

"Hi, this is Chantal. Thank you for calling."

"Hi, this is Reinhard," a male voice rasped on the other end of the line.

This would probably be over fast. "Reinhard. You sound like a really randy stud. Please tell me I can be your mare." Christina whispered and moaned into the phone while she folded the laundry she'd taken from the drier. She stopped mid-motion when she heard the caller moan loudly. This guy had definitely been the fastest today. "Reinhard, don't tell me you just came without me?" Christina gave her voice a disappointed tone.

There was no answer. Instead, the caller hung up.

"Great. A few more calls like that tonight and I've got enough money for a chocolate bar." Christina had been in a bad mood for a while. For three weeks to be exact. Since she'd had this thing with Linda.

Linda. Christina allowed her thoughts to wander to the dark-haired beauty. There wasn't a day, maybe not even an hour, when she didn't think of Linda.

She hadn't wanted to leave. At the airport, she had thought about turning around and driving back. But what then? Linda had paid her—and paid her well—for what had happened between them. And it had been just sex. Right?

Right. But then why did her thoughts stray to Linda again and again?

Amazingly, she didn't feel used at all. Only once had she felt bad: on the day after she'd returned to Cologne, when she had picked up the five thousand euros at the lawyer's office. She didn't feel as if she had done any-thing to deserve that money. Jesus, as often as Linda had brought her to orgasm, Christina should have paid her, not the other way around. Linda's embraces had been wonderful, and her kisses ... oh, the woman could really kiss. Sometimes so tender that Christina couldn't help getting lost in the kiss, and sometimes with a passion that set her whole body on fire.

Christina's lids fluttered shut. Linda's face appeared

before her mind's eye. Standing before her, half-dressed. Shy and yet determined. Or the expression on her face when she came. How she had covered her eyes during the scary scenes in the movie, or licking her spoon when she had eaten ice cream.

Christina opened her eyes and shook her head. She wasn't a teenager in love. For one thing, she was over thirty, and for another, she wasn't in love. It just wasn't possible. She hadn't even spent twenty-four hours with the woman, and for most of the time, they hadn't even talked. Love at first sight didn't exist. Why was she even thinking about it? What was done, was done.

Christina shook her head and continued to fold her laundry. She hoped she would get another, more lucrative call soon.

* * *

"And then there's Christian."

Linda blinked. "Who?"

Her patient, Miriam Behringer, looked at her over the top of her glasses. "Christian. My boyfriend."

"Ah, yes. Of course. What about him?" Linda's thoughts had, as they often did in the last few weeks, returned to Christina, and for a second, she had thought Ms. Behringer had said "Christina." *Focus, dammit.*

"Last night. We had just ... um, you know ... when he looked at me and said, 'Next time I want to be on top. You put on a lot of weight.'"

Linda kept her face expressionless even though she had noticed how much weight her young patient had gained in the last few months, mainly because of her love affair with Ben & Jerry's ice cream. "How did you feel when he said that?"

The patient noisily blew her nose; then she stared at Linda. "How would you have felt?"

"Hurt, I guess."

Ms. Behringer crossed her arms over her chest. "Yes. That's how I felt."

Linda leaned back in her chair. "And what did you do?"

"I went and got myself some ice-cream from the kitchen. Then I felt better."

Oh, great. Linda resisted the urge to roll her eyes. "We've talked about this before," Linda said in a calm, professional tone. "You know the ice-cream is just a substitute for something else."

Ms. Behringer gestured wildly. "I know. But it tastes good, and it helps me calm down."

"What else calms you down?"

"Nothing."

Linda took a deep breath. "What did you do in the past when you were stressed? Before you started eating ice-cream to relax."

Ms. Behringer pouted. "I don't know."

Linda leaned forward, reached for her mug, and took a large sip of tea. Sometimes she thought that Ms. Behringer didn't want any help. Repeatedly, she dug in her heels. "Think about it carefully." Her gaze fell onto the clock above the door. "Oh, our time is up. Please try to remember what relaxed you in the past. Do we have an appointment set up?"

"Yes. Seven p.m. again, next week on Thursday."

"Great. Drive carefully."

Ms. Behringer nodded.

Both stood, and Linda shook her patient's hand. Then

she escorted Ms. Behringer to the door and was finally alone in the office.

As she had often done in the past month whenever she didn't work, her thoughts drifted to Christina. What was she doing right now? Was she working? Was having phone sex the same for Christina as being paid for real sex? *Nonsense. Of course, it's different. Isn't it?*

Christina seemed to enjoy their time together as much as Linda had. On the other hand, Linda couldn't know what was going on inside her head. She told herself all the time that her longing for Christina was actually a longing for closeness and sex. Linda shook her head. *You're just like your patients. You're lying to yourself.* She missed Christina. Her laughter, her gaze, her way of walking and talking, and her playfulness. In between making love, they had joked around, and Linda missed that too. How could a few hours with a stranger affect her so much and throw her life completely off track?

* * *

Groaning, Christina dropped her backpack next to the chest of drawers and kicked the door closed. "God, I thought this day would never end," she murmured while she strolled into the kitchen and threw the mail onto the table. Moaning, she dropped onto the chair next to it. She couldn't go on like this. Last night had been lucrative, but one hour of sleep was definitely too little to make it through a full day of school. *I should take it easy. With Linda's money, I could work less for a while.* Linda. What was she doing right now?

Christina flinched when her cell phone rang. Clumsily, she fumbled around until she had pulled it from her pants pocket that was a bit too tight. "Yes?"

"Hi, Chris, it's Maike."

Christina peeked at the clock. *We just saw each other twenty minutes ago. What does she want?* "Hi. What's up?"

"I just took a look at the math homework. Do you know how to do exercise four?"

Christina almost groaned loudly. Who the hell cared about this crap? "I don't know. I just came in." *And there's a cozy bed waiting for me, so go and bother someone else with this shit.*

"Oh, well, I haven't really gotten started either. Want me to come over later so we can do the homework together?"

Christina stared at her cell phone. Was that a joke? What part of "sorry, you're not my type" had Maike not understood earlier during lunch break? "No, I ... I can't. I have to work."

"Oh, what kind of work do you do?"

Shit. "Um, I work in a call center."

"Cool, my uncle works in a c—"

"Sorry, Maike, I have to go. See you tomorrow, okay?"

Silence.

"Maike?"

"Yeah, sure. See you tomorrow."

"Yep. Until tomorrow." Christina ended the call. *God, what a pain in the ass.* She stuffed the cell phone back into her pant pocket and took the pile of mail from the kitchen table. Advertising, advertising, postcard from Aunt Liselotte, advertising, a letter from a lawyer? She had gotten Linda's money from this lawyer. What did he want? Linda had paid him, hadn't she? Quickly, she opened the envelope. It held two letters. The first one was from the lawyer, saying that the other "party to the contract" wanted to send her a message. With trembling hands, she pulled out the other letter and read:

Dear Christina,

I hope you don't feel this letter is harassment. I didn't call you because I was afraid you'd think I am pestering you. If you don't answer, I won't try to contact you again.

The reason I'm writing you this letter is that I can't forget you. We had so little time together, and I wish I could have gotten to know you better. You seem to be a special woman, and it would be a great honor for me if I could treat you to dinner or coffee.

If you want, you can call me: 030 4673966.
I would love to hear from you.

If you don't want to get in contact with me, I'll accept it, but I want to let you know that the time with you meant a lot to me and I'll never forget you.

Linda

Christina stared at the letter without moving. Finally, she read it again. And again. Then she laid the letter on the table.

* * *

Ring. Ring. Ring. Linda stumbled to the phone. *That has got to be her. She got the letter three days ago. Maybe even four. Yes, I'm sure that's her. Stay cool.* She inhaled and exhaled deeply. With a trembling hand, she picked up the phone. "Linda Klemens."

"Hi, this is Hannah Bäcker."

Linda closed her eyes for a moment and then opened them again. She sank onto the couch. "Hello, Mrs. Bäcker, what can I do for you?"

"I have to cancel our appointment on Monday. My babysitter broke her ankle and can't watch Mia."

"I see." Linda reached for her calendar on the coffee table. "That's no problem. When exactly is the appointment?"

"At three."

She took the pen that was clipped to the calendar and crossed out the appointment. "Okay. Call me when you have more time. I'm sure we can make an appointment when the little one is in kindergarten."

"Thank you, Ms. Klemens."

"How are you doing?"

"It's not easy. Mia isn't sleeping through the night. And I'm quite quick-tempered right now."

"Did you think about my suggestion?"

Mrs. Bäcker sighed. "I'm not sure that's a good idea. He never gave me any attention."

Linda plucked lint from her sweater. "It's your decision."

"But you think I should let Mia see her father," Mrs. Bäcker said.

"She hasn't seen him for several weeks. From what you told me about him, he always treated Mia lovingly, and it seems your daughter misses her father." Normally, she was careful not to openly state her opinion, but this time, she couldn't help herself. Maybe it was unprofessional, but to keep a child from her father just because the parents' marriage failed ... Linda closed her eyes. No child should have to miss their parents.

Mrs. Bäcker was quiet. After some time, she said, "I'll think about it."

Linda opened her eyes. *This isn't about you. Get yourself together.* "Being a single mom isn't easy, but as far as I can see, you're doing a good job."

"Thanks."

Linda stood. "Call me if you need me or when you want to set up a new appointment. I'm sure we'll find a solution."

"I don't know what I'd do without you."

"You'd do just fine. You can be proud of how you cope with things every day."

"Thanks again. Good night, Ms. Klemens."

"Good night." Linda ended the call and strolled into the kitchen. She took a glass from the cupboard and filled it with water from the tap. She shook her head. Recently, she was much more emotional than usual, wasn't she? She took a big sip.

The phone rang. *Christina!* Linda put the glass down abruptly, ran to the living room, and snatched the cordless phone from the coffee table. "Linda Klemens."

"Good evening. My name is Lasser," a female voice said. "I'm calling on behalf of Sedacom. We have a new product that I'd like to introduce you to. It's a—"

"Ms. Lasser." Linda took a deep breath. "The bailiff has already been here twice to take my furniture, and I'm facing insolvency. If your product isn't free, I'm afraid I have to decline."

Everything was silent on the other end of the line. A click and the line went dead.

Linda grinned and put the phone down. *It works every time.* As soon as she had put the phone down, it started to ring again. *It's not boring today.* "Linda Klemens."

Someone breathed quietly but frantically on the other end of the line.

Linda lifted one brow. "Hello?"

Still nothing.

Was it a patient? Maybe Mrs. Gänzler. She had seemed very unstable during their last session. "Is everything okay?"

"It's Christina." Her voice shook.

Linda stared at the cold hardwood floor beneath her equally cold feet. She had waited for this call. Again and again, she had gone through this situation in her mind. She had planned every word she would say. But now her head was blank. Completely blank.

"Linda?"

She cleared her throat. "I'm here." *Do I sound hoarse?*

For a moment, both were silent until Christina asked, "Am I calling at a bad time?"

"No. No. It's nice of you to call. How are you?" Linda sank onto the couch and tucked her ice-cold feet under her thighs.

"I'm fine." After pausing, Christina said, "I got your letter."

God, what do I say to that? "Yes, of course you did. How else would you know my phone number"? No. "Great, how is it going?" No. Linda bit her lower lip. *Keep calm.* "I'm glad you called."

Rustling echoed through the phone, then Christina said, "I was surprised to hear from you."

What can I answer? Linda's gaze darted across the room. *The truth. Just tell her the truth.* "I couldn't forget you."

Silence.

"I couldn't forget you either," Christina said quietly.

Linda's heart pounded in her ears. "Can I invite you to dinner?"

"You're in Berlin, and I'm in Cologne."

Linda smiled. "I could fly down next weekend and stay the night." When no answer came, she added hastily, "I will stay at a hotel, of course."

Something creaked. "I don't know."

Slowly, Linda blew out the breath she'd held. Christina had called her, so there was a chance for them. *Careful. Don't rush it.* "How about this: We speak on the phone for now to get to know each other a little better. We're not in any hurry. And then you can decide if you want to see me again. Um, if I may invite you to dinner. What do you think?"

Again, there was only this awful silence. The ticking of the clock behind her was almost deafening.

"Okay."

Linda beamed. *Yes!* "Do you have some time to talk now, or do you have to work?"

"I'm calling from my private line. As long as the second line doesn't ring, I can talk."

"I see. So ..." Linda's fingers drummed against the back of the couch. Normally, she didn't have any problems starting a conversation with other people. It was part of her job. But now, with Christina, she had no clue how to keep the conversation going.

Christina cleared her throat. "What are you doing right now?"

"I ... I'm sitting on the couch in the living room, talking on the phone."

Christina giggled. "And what were you doing before I called?"

Smiling, Linda said, "I got rid of a phone saleswoman, and before that, a patient called. She had to cancel an appointment."

"Do your patients often call you at home?"

"It happens. Mainly to set up appointments, but sometimes I get calls because a patient is going through a crisis."

"Mmhh, that means you're on call twenty-four/seven. That has to be pretty stressful."

Linda shrugged. "Not really. It's not like I get calls every hour. And in the two years since I've opened my own practice, I've only gotten one call at night."

"At night?"

"Yes. It was an emergency. Directly after the call, the patient had to go to the hospital."

"Oh."

Linda rolled her eyes. *Don't bore her with your job.* "Enough about me. What are you doing right now?"

"I'm sitting on my bed, talking to you on the phone."

Linda grinned. "Really?"

"Mmhhmm."

"What else?"

"I tried to do my math homework, but I'm really bad at math."

"Math?" *Yes! She's telling me details about her private life.*

"Yep. I'm getting my Abitur."

Oh. "I see. Mmhh … What subjects are you covering right now? I was pretty good at math. Maybe I can help."

"I started school not too long ago. We're just going over the basics right now. But I only finished Hauptschule, so the stuff we're doing now isn't so easy for me. And it's been a long time."

Linda lifted her hand to her mouth but stopped herself at the last moment. She had stopped chewing her nails years ago. *Should I ask about her life story or try to help her with homework instead? She'll tell you more about herself if she wants to. I hope.* Linda fumbled with the seam of her pants. Helping Christina would get her more brownie points, so she decided to do that. "What's the problem?"

"Do you have something to write?"

"No. Give me a minute." The phone still held to her ear, Linda jumped up, hurried to her office, and turned on the light. She took a few sheets of paper from the desk drawer and took a pen from the penholder before she dropped onto her desk chair. "Shoot."

"$4x^2$ divided by $3x^2$ plus $5x$ minus, um, 3 equals $7x$."

"Okay, I've got it. What exactly are you having difficulties with?"

"I don't understand this stuff." A creaking sound reverberated through the phone. It sounded as if Christina was getting more comfortable on her bed.

An image of Christina sleeping in her bed shot through Linda's mind. Naked and barely covered by a blanket. Her mouth went dry, and she swallowed. *Focus. Jesus.* Since Christina's visit a few weeks ago, she kept flashing back to memories of their time together. But now wasn't the time to daydream.

"I've got no clue how to approach this. I know it's something basic. We just got started on this subject, but I just don't know how to solve the equation."

Linda studied the equation. "Okay, the good news is, I can help you. So ..."

Ring. Ring. Ring.

"Damn, a client. I'm sorry."

Linda blinked. How could she have forgotten what Christina did for a living? "No problem. Want me to wait?"

"Do you really want to listen? I can call you back or ..."

The phone rang again.

"Pick up. I'll wait."

"Okay." Christina cleared her throat and then said, "Hi, this is Chantal. Thank you for calling ... Hello, Friedrich. Tell me what you want to do to me."

Linda had forgotten that voice. Goose bumps broke out all over her body, and an image of Christina's seductive body flashed through her mind's eye.

"Oh, yes, that sounds good. Tell me more ... Oh, yes."

Linda clutched the phone more firmly. She hung on every word that Christina breathed or moaned. God, she wanted this woman.

Christina was silent.

Apparently, the client said something. The thought jerked Linda back into reality. Christina was talking to a man. A man who was most likely masturbating. Suddenly, Linda felt nauseated. She stood and got a glass of water from the kitchen. She took a big sip, then nearly inhaled it when Christina said, "I'm so wet already, oh, yes, take your time. Yes, exactly like that." The words were more moaned then spoken.

Maybe it was childish, but Linda wished she could interrupt the call somehow. This man didn't deserve to talk to Christina. She was so much more than a—

"More. Harder. Uhhh."

Linda gritted her teeth. Her body betrayed her. She felt herself become wet. She marched into the living room and banged her half-full glass onto the coffee table. A few drops spilled over. While she took a tissue and wiped down the table, she put the phone aside. Christina's normal voice was much more attractive. And the men who ... Linda took a deep breath. The men who called her didn't get to listen to the real Christina, to the voice that enchanted with its mix of vulnerability and strength. That one belonged just to her. *Belongs to me? Don't be ridiculous.* She had to come to her senses. Gritting her teeth, she picked up the phone again.

"Oh, yes ... yessss."

Linda had to swallow. Christina apparently really enjoyed her work. How could she—?

"You know how to really give it to a woman." Christina moaned. "Harder? Oh, yes, you really know what I like. Yessss ... mmhh ... yes ... yes ... yes."

Linda opened her eyes wide. Had Christina lied to her? Was she straight after all? *What am I doing here? I don't know her at all.*

"That was so good, baby," Christina whispered. "Please tell me I'll get more of you later." After a short silence, Christina said, "That's what I wanted to hear, sweetie. Until later. I'll wait for your call."

Linda lifted the glass of water and emptied it in one big gulp. *Admit it. You're aroused.* She tapped her finger against the empty glass. Maybe she was aroused, but at the same time ... She didn't know what she felt, but it was definitely not a good feeling.

Someone cleared her throat on the other end of the line. "Linda?"

"Yes?" *Was that my voice?* Linda sounded hoarse. She coughed.

"You okay? I'm sorry it took so long." Christina sounded entirely normal now. The versatility of her voice was amazing.

It's her job. That's all. At least Linda hoped that was all it was. "No problem. Uh, where were we?"

"The equation. I thought about it during the call. Can I cancel the $4x^2$ against the $3x^2$?"

Linda furrowed her brow. "You thought about math during the call?"

"I couldn't do anything but math," Christina said. "I had already folded and ironed the laundry, and the batteries of the cordless are dead, so I had to use the phone here and couldn't leave the bedroom. What else should I have done?"

Linda's mouth fell open.

Christina laughed. "Did you think I'm imagining sleeping with a guy? Or that the call turns me on?"

"Uh … uhm …"

"I hate to disappoint you. For one thing, I'm not bi, and secondly, my role as Chantal turns me on about as much as watching the news."

It felt as if a lead apron had been lifted off Linda's shoulders. She breathed deeply. First, she smiled, and then she started to laugh. *I'm an idiot.* "I've got to give you that, Christina. You sound really hot."

"Thanks."

Linda put her glass on the coffee table, leaned back, and stared off into space. *She's a great actress. I wonder if she ...?* After pausing, Linda asked, "Was it also just an act with me?"

Christina said nothing.

God, what are you doing? Don't remind her that you were a ... Linda swallowed. *... customer too.* As much as she wanted to know the answer, it was much too soon for the question. "I'm sorry. Forget what I said."

After a moment that seemed to last forever, Christina said, "I canceled down the $4x^2$ against the $3x^2$. What do I do now?"

She let me off the hook. In the future, Linda would choose her words more carefully. She reached for the sheet of paper with the equation. "Okay, let's solve this together."

* * *

"Klemens."

"What are you doing right now?"

Linda grinned. "Hi, Christina. Good evening to you too. What? How am I doing? I'm fine, and how are you?"

"Stop it. I need your advice."

Linda plopped down onto the couch. "Ah. What for?"

Something rustled on the other end of the line. "I've got a date to go see a musical in half an hour, and I don't know what to wear."

Linda's stomach suddenly felt as if she had swallowed a brick. "You ... you've got a date?"

"Mmhh?"

"A date. You said you've got ..."

"Yes. My sister gave me tickets to a musical for my birthday."

Sister? Linda breathed a sigh of relief. Christina wasn't going out with some woman; she just had a date with her sister. *Wait a minute.* "You've got a sister?"

"Two. One younger, one older."

"Ah. I see. You said she invited you to the musical for your birthday. When ...?"

"Could we focus on my problem for now?" The rustling echoed through the phone again.

Is she getting undressed? An image of Christina's naked body flashed through Linda's mind. Heat swept through her. *Focus.* "Uh, sure. So, what choices do you have?"

"An anthracite pant suit with a white blouse or ... or a gray blouse. That one's got a lower neckline. Mmhh, I could also wear the pants of the pantsuit and my Bordeaux-red wool sweater. Oh, I don't know."

Linda smiled. They had talked on the phone for five evenings in a row. At first, she had worried when Christina had said she wouldn't be able to talk to her tonight. But now that they were talking, it was like a warm summer rain. Christina was much more relaxed now than on the first evening. "It all sounds good. Why don't you wear the wool sweater. By the time the musical is finished, it will be cold outside."

"You're right. Hold on." A crackling sound, then the line went silent. After what felt like an eternity, the sound came again and then a panting Christina said, "Okay. I put it on."

"And?" Linda asked. "Do you like it?"

"Yes. I think you're right. I would freeze in one of the blouses."

"What will you see?"

"What?"

"Which musical will you see."

"Oh, *Shadowland*."

"Ah." Linda rubbed her neck. "I don't know that one."

"Silvia says it's great."

"Is Silvia your sister?"

"Yep, my little sister." Christina's voice reverberated through the phone. She was probably in the bathroom now.

"How much younger is she?"

"Silvia is one and a half years younger and Astrid almost four years older than me."

"Having siblings must be nice," Linda said quietly.

After a few moments, Christina asked, her voice serious, "You're an only child, right?"

"Yes."

"I can't imagine being an only child. My sisters have always been there. Without them ... I don't know. It wouldn't be the same." The shrill ringing of a doorbell made Linda flinch. "That's Silvia. Good timing. Thanks for your help. You're a lifesaver. No matter if it's about math homework or choosing the right outfit."

"My pleasure. Enjoy your evening."

"Thanks. You too. Bye."

"Until soon." Linda ended the call but still held the phone in her hand. They had talked for just a few minutes, but Linda's mood had improved one hundred percent. She sighed. Christina was a cutie.

* * *

Christina dropped onto the bed, phone in hand. Her homework was done, dinner eaten, and the second phone line disconnected. Tonight, she would allow herself the luxury of not working. Quickly, she dialed Linda's number. Her heart beat like a drum, as it had every day for the last two weeks.

"Klemens."

"Hi. Am I calling at a bad time?"

"Never," Linda said. "How are you? How was your day?"

"We didn't have math today. In other words: I had a great day. How about you?"

"Pretty much the same as usual."

"Pretty much?" Christina sipped her coke.

Linda laughed. "It's almost scary how well you know me by now."

The bed creaked as Christina turned onto her belly. "You think so?"

"Absolutely."

"Linda?"

"Yes?"

"You still haven't answered my question."

Linda laughed again. "I can't hide anything from you." Sobering, she said, "I'm worried about a patient of mine. That's all."

"Do you want to talk about it?"

"I want to, but I'm bound to confidentiality."

Christina grunted. "I don't know his name or how he looks or anything."

Linda was quiet for a long time and then said, "He's been suffering from depression for years. Sometimes, he's a little better, but never for long. He has become withdrawn in the past few weeks. He refuses to take any medication. If he's not better next week, I'll urge him to go to the hospital."

"A psychiatric ward?"

"Yes."

"Can't you admit him?"

"No," Linda said. "I'm a psychologist, not a psychiatrist."

"Oh, I see."

"But enough about work. I realized you hardly ever talk about yourself."

Christina stiffened. Was it that obvious? "There's not much to tell."

"I don't want to interrogate you, and you can tell me if there's something you don't want to talk about."

"But?" Christina sat up and leaned against the head-rest of her bed.

"Would it bother you if I ask you a few questions?"

Christina hesitated. They hardly knew each other. *That's not the reason, and you know it.* Her feelings for Linda were conflicted. After all, Linda was her ... Christina swallowed. She had been her john. *You never saw her like that. You can lie to the whole world, but don't lie to yourself.* She liked Linda. She liked her very much. But opening up to her would only create problems. Relationships ended in pain. It had always been that way, and she and Linda never had a chance. It had been a mistake to call her after getting the letter. Exactly. It would be best if she ended it now before—

"It's okay if you don't want to talk about yourself. Really."

Linda's gentle voice wrecked her determination in a split second. "Uh, what do you want to know?" Christina asked.

"What's your favorite color?"

"What?"

"Your favorite color."

"Oh." That was all? "Uh, red. Bordeaux-red. And yours?"

"Black."

Christina snorted. "Black is not a color."

"Sure it is. Otherwise you couldn't see it."

"Well, you can't when it's dark."

"When it's dark, you can't see any color."

Christina rolled her eyes. "I give up. Do you have any other question?"

"How come you're getting your Abitur at thirty?"

"Wow, now you're getting daring."

"You don't want to talk about favorite colors, so what else is there?"

Christina laughed loudly. "You're incorrigible, you know?"

"To be honest, you're the first one to tell me that."

Christina heard a crunching sound. "What are you eating?"

"Chips," Linda mumbled. "You've got to spoil yourself sometimes." Again, the chips crunched.

"I didn't have any formal job training after I finished Hauptschule. I started working in a factory that made cakes. The factory went bankrupt, and I lost my job. Since I don't have any other skills, I didn't find a job. There were too many other people with a good education. The job center told me to go back to school and get the Abitur. That's the whole story." Christina held her breath. Now she had said it. She had no degree and no job training. How would Linda react?

"I admire you. Others might have just leaned back and done nothing. You don't get any unemployment benefits, do you?"

She admires me? Had she heard correctly? Linda didn't think she was a total loser? "No, and I'm too old to get financial aid from the state for going back to school. That's why I do ... the phone job."

"I see." After pausing, Linda asked, "Is it hard for you?"

Christina shrugged. "The first few calls were hard. But I learned quickly to turn off my brain. Since then, it's easy money."

Silence.

Christina closed her eyes. "Do you think I'm a bad person because I ...?"

"What? No. God, no."

Slowly, Christina opened her eyes. "What is it, then?"

"I don't think I could do that. That's all. I respect you for wanting to get a better education and for doing things that are ... um ... unpleasant for you to achieve your goals."

She really means it. Christina hadn't been expecting that. So far, her friends had told her she was crazy when she mentioned going back to school. "The constant lack of sleep is the worst thing. School during the day and the job at night. That's exhausting."

"I can imagine," Linda said.

"But there is no other way. Doesn't matter. Let's talk about you. Why did you become a psychologist? Why not become a physician or lawyer?"

Linda laughed. "I can't stand the sight of blood, and studying law books is not my idea of fun." Her tone became serious. "My mother was a psychologist."

"Oh. Did she want you to follow in her footsteps?"

"She left it up to me. But I wanted to be like her. My father was a lawyer, but that didn't appeal to me."

"What's so great about psychology?"

"People."

"People?"

"Yes. The way they think, the way they feel. Every human being is a big mystery. One that can never be solved completely. Do you know what I mean?"

"I never looked at it that way. But I think I know what you mean."

"Okay, let's talk about something much more important." The bag of chips rustled on the other end of the line.

"What's that?"

"If you worked in a cake factory, does that mean you know how to make delicious cakes? I love cheesecake."

Christina laughed. Linda really was incorrigible.

* * *

Yawning, Linda glanced at the wall clock in the living room. She and Christina had been talking for over four hours now. Their conversation was everything but boring. For the last month, they had talked nearly every evening, and they had never run out of topics to discuss. But now it was after one in the morning, and her alarm clock would be ringing at six. "I think it's time for me to turn in. My first appointment tomorrow is at seven."

Christina was silent, then said, "You work too much."

Linda stood and rubbed her eyes while she trudged to the kitchen. "You do too."

"You can't compare my job to yours. I have to listen to panting guys come while I breath dumb sentences into the phone. You have to focus and deal with the thoughts and emotions of other people."

"I like my job."

"I don't doubt that, but maybe you should work fewer hours."

"What am I supposed to do instead?" Linda smiled.

After a long silence, Christina said quietly, "Come to Cologne."

Linda was about to pour herself a glass of water. As if in slow motion, she put down the water bottle. "Do you mean that?"

"Yes."

Linda's heart pounded. "When?"

Christina chuckled.

"Seriously. When do you want me to come?"

"This weekend is probably too short notice."

"No, it isn't." Linda hurried into her office. "Give me a second. I'll boot up the computer, book the flight and a hotel room. Anything you can recommend? A hotel, I mean."

"Uh, not really. I never needed a hotel here."

"Makes sense."

A few minutes later, she had booked a flight and a hotel room. "We can meet on Saturday afternoon or evening. What do you prefer?"

"When do you arrive?"

"My flight lands at Cologne/Bonn airport a little after three p.m."

"Want me ... want me to pick you up?"

Linda wanted to jump with joy. She couldn't believe her good fortune. "If you want to. I'd like that."

"Give me your flight number and your arrival time. I'll be there."

* * *

Linda shifted in her seat. The airplane would land in a few minutes. Even though they were flying lower now, everything on the ground still seemed so far away. As far away as her life before Christina. She couldn't imagine how her life had been without Christina. Before, she would never have talked about her work, but now she did every night. Christina always told her about her day at school and occasionally, she talked about her family.

Not an hour went by that Linda didn't think of Christina and how at ease they were with each other now. Everything had changed. She glanced at her wristwatch and swallowed. Just a little longer. How would they greet each other? A handshake? An embrace? A kiss? What were they to each other? Christina occasionally called her "sweetie" and sometimes even "beautiful." Apart from that, they flirted only in a very subtle way and kept their conversations platonic. But that was on the phone. *When we see each other again, things will be different, won't they?*

* * *

Christina shifted her weight from one leg to the other. Linda would arrive any moment now. And then what? Had inviting her been the right thing to do? Silly question. With every day that went by, her longing for Linda grew. She longed for her touch, her smell, her smile. But ... *It will never work.* Once they met face to face, the illusion of closeness that had formed on the phone would disappear. *Yes. That's what will happen.*

A door opened, and the first passengers departed. None of them was Linda.

Christina rubbed her ice-cold hands. *Calm. Keep*

calm. But her racing heart had other plans.

And then, suddenly, she was there. Linda hesitantly passed the automatic doors, pulling a small suitcase. She looked in Christina's direction and stopped as if lightning had hit her. Slowly, she moved toward Christina and stopped four feet away.

Christina's body tingled and felt as if it were a magnet that was pulled toward Linda, but she resisted and didn't move.

"Hi." Linda's voice shook.

"Hi." Christina exhaled noisily. *To hell with it.* She took one step forward and wrapped her arms around Linda.

Linda returned the embrace.

Christina held her tightly. After some time, she let go and smiled. "We should go."

Linda nodded.

Wordlessly, they walked toward the parking garage.

As they approached her sixteen-year-old Ford Fiesta, Christina wanted to dig a hole and hide. Linda was used to much better cars. *I hope it will start.* Earlier, it had taken almost a full minute before the engine had come to life. She unlocked the passenger side door, took Linda's suitcase, and managed to open the trunk. With a low grunt, she stowed the suitcase, then closed the trunk with as much force as possible. After testing the lid, she happily realized that it stayed shut for a change. She hurried around the car.

Linda had already gotten in on the passenger side.

When Christina saw Linda with her long legs perched in her little car, hanging halfway across the dashboard, she didn't know if she should laugh or cry. "You can move the seat back a little. The lever is beneath the seat," she said instead.

Linda glanced up at her, smiled in a way that looked pained, and then the passenger seat wobbled back, screeching and creaking.

The seat was now as far back as it would go.

"Maybe you could ..."

Linda lifted one hand. "No, it's fine. It's not all that, um, uncomfortable. Really. I'll manage."

Christina lifted her brows. She better get going, or Linda would be forced to sit like this even longer. Christina slid into the driver's seat. The car rocked a little, but Christina ignored it and turned the key in the ignition. The engine started without a problem. She exhaled. Finally, something was going right.

They were silent on the way to the hotel. Christina didn't know what to say, and Linda stared at her knees as if she had been hypnotized. From time to time, Christina looked at her, and sometimes she thought she had felt Linda's gaze on her. *Say something. Come on. Say something.* "Uh, I think the hotel where you booked a room is a good one."

Abruptly, Linda turned her head in her direction. "Really?"

No idea. I just wanted to say something. No, she couldn't say that. Christina looked back at the street in front of her. "Mmhh."

After reaching the hotel, Christina lifted the suitcase out of the trunk and handed it over to Linda. *Let's get out of here. For one day, I babbled enough nonsense.* "I'll pick you up at seven, so you've got enough time to freshen up, okay?"

Linda waited next to the car, the suitcase in front of her like a shield, and nodded.

"We'll eat at *Le Patron* if that's okay. It's supposed to be a really good French restaurant."

"Sounds ... sounds good. I like French."

Mmhh, I noticed. Christina mentally shook her head. *God, get yourself together.* "Well, then ... then I'll see you later."

The corners of Linda's mouth twitched. "Sure. See you later."

Hastily, Christina got in and drove off. She hoped the evening would go better.

* * *

With one trembling hand, Christina brushed a strand of hair from her face while she craned her neck and stared in the rearview mirror. Was all of this a mistake? Linda was still a woman who had paid her for sex. What if all Linda wanted was to get the same thing for free? *Maybe she's not as emotionally involved as ... as me.* Christina shook her head. Linda definitely wanted more than sex. Right? Right. And what would be so bad about having incredible sex again? Christina grinned about her thoughts. This whole situation was strange.

A knock at the window made her look up.

Linda stood in front of the locked passenger side door.

Christina leaned over and opened the door.

Smiling shyly, Linda slid onto the passenger seat and smoothed her hands over her tight mini skirt.

Christina loved how she looked in it. The skirt ended just above her knees. Normally, Linda didn't wear skirts or dresses. *She's wearing it just for me.* The blue silk blouse, the shoes with semi-high heels, and the purse all matched perfectly. What little makeup Linda wore emphasized her natural beauty. She looked amazingly good.

Christina's mouth went dry. As much as she tried not to stare, she couldn't help herself.

"Good evening."

Christina swallowed. "Good evening."

Linda fiddled with her skirt and then clutched her purse so tightly that her knuckles went white.

Sighing quietly, Christina turned away, started the car, and pulled out into traffic. She hated the awkwardness that suddenly existed between them.

Linda cleared her throat. "You look good."

"Thanks, you too," Christina said. Linda looked more than good. When Christina stopped at a red light, she peeked at the beauty next to her again. Their gazes met.

Someone honked behind Christina.

She wrenched her gaze away from Linda and crossed the intersection.

"You look good in pantsuits," Linda said.

God, she sounds so sexy. Christina looked down at herself. She rarely wore this pantsuit, but she had tried not to dress too provocatively. This was a dinner between friends, not foreplay for wanton sex. Christina swallowed. No, sex wasn't on the menu. She would focus on Linda's face, so her thoughts wouldn't stray in that direction.

"Have you been to this restaurant before?" Linda asked.

A shiver ran down Christina's spine. *Okay, and talking might not be such a good idea either.* The thought made her grin and shake her head. "Definitely not," she said, smiling.

"What's so funny?"

"Normally this restaurant is a bit out of my league ... or that of my paycheck. But I think it'll fit your exquisite tastes."

Linda's expression hardened. "I don't care where we're going. I care about who I eat with, not how many stars the restaurant has."

Christina gritted her teeth. *I guess that backfired on me.*

"Let's go somewhere else. I'm sure there are some good, but more affordable restaurants."

Exhaling loudly, Christina said, "I reserved a table for us. And I want to take you to the best restaurant in Cologne, not just a good one."

"The price doesn't necessarily tell you something about the quality of the food."

Christina said nothing.

Linda clicked her tongue. "Then at least allow me to pay."

"No." Christina's answer came fast and sounded harsher than intended. "You're my guest tonight."

Both were silent for a long time.

Linda shifted in her seat. After some time, she said in a serious tone, "We'll go Dutch, okay?"

When they reached the restaurant, Christina shut off the engine and studied Linda insistently. *She knows I don't have much money. She's trying to make things easier for me. Get over yourself.* "Okay."

But neither of them got out of the car. Instead, they silently stared at each other. Christina couldn't stop admiring Linda's beauty—her shining eyes, the long legs, and the full breasts. Everything about her seemed to be perfect. But Linda's beauty was so much more than skin-deep.

"I missed you," Linda whispered. While she was speaking, she reached out her hand to touch Christina's cheek but stopped an inch or two away. Linda lowered her hand and put it in her lap.

Me too. Christina didn't voice her thought. It was all moving too fast. Instead, she reached for Linda's hand and lifted it to her cheek. The heat Linda radiated seemed to engulf Christina's whole body. How she'd missed this. She barely resisted the urge to close her eyes. "Let's go in."

Linda nodded, and they got out of the car.

Christina locked the doors and walked over to Linda. Now that she was standing, Linda looked even more seductive. *Look at her face. Just her face.* But, damn, even that was irresistible with that sweet smile and the shy gaze. Christina offered her arm, and Linda slipped hers through it. Side by side, they entered the restaurant.

* * *

Their table was in the middle of the large restaurant. Numerous other guests were seated all around them. While most of them were engrossed in lively conversation, Linda and Christina remained silent. After each had ordered a glass of red wine, they studied the menu.

Christina had to grin.

"What's so funny?" Linda asked. Obviously, she had watched Christina.

Shaking her head, Christina looked up. "I don't have an appetite again. Seems to be the norm whenever we have dinner together."

Linda laughed, first quietly, then more loudly until the people at the surrounding tables looked over at her.

"I'm not hungry either."

Both laughed until tears formed in their eyes.

But when the laughter ceased, silence settled around them again.

Oh, come on. This is Linda. We wanted to spend a nice evening together. It can't be that hard to have a conversation. If you weren't in a restaurant but at home, talking on the phone, we would talk until the batteries are dead or we fall asleep out of sheer exhaustion. But as much as she wanted to, not a single word came out of her mouth.

After they ordered, Linda took a big sip of the red wine the waiter had poured for them, and slowly put down the glass. "It's strange how few intelligent thoughts you have when your feelings go crazy."

Christina wordlessly stared at Linda. *She wants to talk about her feelings?* "What do you feel?"

"For you?"

Christina's heart was in her mouth. Was she ready for the answer? It didn't matter. There was no way back. She nodded.

"Do you believe in love at first sight?" Linda asked quietly.

Uh. What had made Linda think of that? Christina held her breath. Was it love that Linda was feeling? *Please, please, please.* Christina inhaled carefully and looked deeply into her eyes. "Do you?"

Linda lowered her gaze and leaned back. Then she looked at Christina with a hint of a smile on her lips. "As a psychologist, I should probably say no."

Should? Christina swallowed.

Linda leaned forward. "I fell in love with you. It happened the first time we met." Linda took Christina's ice-cold hand in hers. "I already felt attracted to you the first time I heard your normal voice. On that first night, before I knew how ... how wonderful you are."

Frozen, Christina stared at her. Her heart pounded frantically, and her mind was totally blank.

"I don't expect anything from you. If you want to give me your friendship, that's enough for me." Linda's trembling hand caressed Christina's motionless fingers. "And if you feel the same, I don't want to pressure you. You hold all the cards."

Christina rolled her eyes and said the first thing that came to mind, "You really know how to take the pressure off someone."

Linda grinned, and Christina followed her lead.

After a while, Christina's smile faded away. She pulled her hand back and put it on her lap. "I don't know what this thing between us is, and I have no idea if there's a chance that we ... that you and I can be more than just friends." Christina shook her head. "We come from two completely different worlds. And don't forget how we met."

Jutting out her chin, Linda said, "I don't care where we came from or how we got here. We're here now. That's the only thing that matters."

Silence.

When the waiter suddenly stood in front of them, Christina flinched. She watched him serve the food, then disappear again.

They ate in silence, the only sounds the clattering of the cutlery on the plates and the quiet conversations at the surrounding tables.

Christina's gaze repeatedly returned to Linda, who stared at her plate as if it presented an interesting puzzle.

This was the moment of truth. She held all the cards. Linda had made it very clear what she felt and wanted. *But what do I want?* She was thirty-one years old. Did she really want to rush into a fling like a teenager?

A fling? No, Linda wasn't asking for a fling. *She's talking about love and deeper feelings for me.* They had gotten to know each other a bit better in the last few weeks. Linda wasn't a person who rushed into things without thinking it through. But still ... what if it didn't work out? *Do I even feel the same?* She knew the answer before she finished the question. There was no doubt about it. She was in love too, more deeply than ever before. "Let's pay and leave."

Linda blinked. "And then?"

"And then I want you to spend the night with me."

Linda's eyes widened. For endless seconds, she sat without moving until she mechanically lifted her hand.

When the waiter walked over, Linda rummaged through her wallet and gave him a few bills. Then she jumped up, reached for Christina's hand, and hurried her out of the restaurant.

* * *

Linda's heart pounded. Every step felt as if she were walking on clouds. Cool air hit her outside of the restaurant. It was refreshing. Wonderful. Everything was wonderful. Christina wanted to give them a chance. Her courage had been rewarded. When they reached the car, she stopped and pulled Christina closer. If she didn't say it now, she'd burst. "I know it sounds crazy, but I love you."

Christina grinned. "It doesn't just sound crazy. It is

crazy. But I love you too."

Their faces moved closer and closer until their lips met in a light kiss. It felt so right. Linda wanted the kiss to never end.

When her cell phone rang, Christina ignored it.

"Don't you want to take the call? It could be important," Linda said.

Christina shook her head. "You called me. That was important." She smiled and took the still ringing cell phone out of her purse. She turned it off and put it away. "Whoever that was can wait until tomorrow. Or the day after tomorrow." She pulled Linda toward the car. "Let's go. I've got plans for tonight."

###

About Alison Grey

Alison has been writing since the age of ten. Her first works were poems and short stories; then she wrote her first novel-length book when she was eleven. It was a *Star Trek: The Next Generation* fanfiction.

In addition to writing, Alison likes spending her spare time with her friends. The vegetarian also loves cooking and baking. If she's got enough time, she reads books about history and about social and political sciences.

E-Mail: Alison-Grey@web.de

Something in the Wine
Jae

Length: 99,100 words (novel)

All her life, Annie Prideaux has suffered through her brother's constant practical jokes only he thinks are funny. But Jake's last joke is one too many, she decides when he sets her up on a blind date with his friend Drew Corbin—neglecting to tell his straight sister one tiny detail: her date is not a man, but a lesbian.

Annie and Drew decide it's time to turn the tables on

Jake by pretending to fall in love with each other.

At first glance, they have nothing in common. Disillusioned with love, Annie focuses on books, her cat, and her work as an accountant while Drew, more confident and outgoing, owns a dog and spends most of her time working in her beloved vineyard.

Only their common goal to take revenge on Jake unites them. But what starts as a table-turning game soon turns Annie's and Drew's lives upside down as the lines between pretending and reality begin to blur.

Something in the Wine is a story about love, friendship, and coming to terms with what it means to be yourself.

Manhattan Moon
Jae

Length: 28,500 words (novella)

Nothing in Shelby Carson's life is ordinary. Not only is she an attending psychiatrist in a hectic ER, but she's also a Wrasa, a shape-shifter who leads a secret existence.

To make things even more complicated, she has feelings for Nyla Rozakis, a human nurse.

Even though the Wrasa forbid relationships with humans, Shelby is determined to pursue Nyla. Things seem pretty hopeless for them, but on Halloween, during a full moon, anything can happen...

Connected Hearts
Jae, RJ Nolan, Joan Arling

Length: 33,000 words

Four romantic short stories:
The Morning After by Jae
After a friend sets her up on a blind date from hell, Amanda has enough of dating. A spur-of-the-moment decision to attend an Anti-Valentine's Day party leads to an unexpected encounter. She wakes up to a hangover and a surprising complication...

Two Hearts—One Mind by RJ Nolan
Kim is a woman on a mission: She wants to propose to her partner, Jess, on Valentine's Day. But things don't turn out as planned, because Jess has a plan of her own...

On the Road by Joan Arling
Stella, a long-haul trucker, picks up a hitchhiker on her way south across Europe. Long before reaching Sicily, she falls for her passenger, Rita. Stella is thrilled when she learns that Rita returns her feelings. But because of her job, there seems to be no way for them to be together.

Seduction for Beginners by Jae
For Annie, work always took precedence over romance. But now, recently come-out and involved in a relationship with a woman for the first time, Annie is determined to seduce her girlfriend, Drew, on Valentine's Day. Unfortunately, she has no clue as to the arts of seduction.

Coming from Ylva Publishing in spring 2013
http://www.ylva-publishing.com

Backwards to Oregon
(revised edition)
Jae

"Luke" Hamilton has always been sure that she'd never marry. She accepted that she would spend her life alone when she chose to live her life disguised as a man.

After working in a brothel for three years, Nora Macauley has lost all illusions about love. She no longer hopes for a man who will sweep her off her feet and take her away to begin a new, respectable life.

But now they find themselves married and on the way to Oregon in a covered wagon, with two thousand miles ahead of them.

L.A. Metro
(second edition)
RJ Nolan

Dr. Kimberly Donovan's life is in shambles. After her medical ethics are questioned, first her family, then her closeted lover, the Chief of the ER, betray her. Determined to make a fresh start, she flees to California and L.A. Metropolitan Hospital.

Dr. Jess McKenna, L.A. Metro's Chief of the ER, gives new meaning to the phrase emotionally guarded, but she has her reasons.

When Kim and Jess meet, the attraction is immediate.

Emotions Jess has tried to repress for years surface. But her interest in Kim also stirs dark memories. They settle for friendship, determined not to repeat past mistakes, but secretly they both wish things could be different.

Will the demons from Jess's past destroy their future before it can even get started? Or will L.A. Metro be a place to not only heal the sick, but to mend wounded hearts?